Some Die Young

Some Die Young

JAMES DUFF

WILDSIDE PRESS

Some Die Young

Published by Wildside Press LLC
www.wildsidepress.com

PART I

The Hidden

1

He tottered on his short legs, fall-ing into the empty chair. His right hand grasped the half-empty bottle with a desperate fierceness. His eyes stared at me, unseeing, and his left hand made a half-hearted attempt at straightening the sparse grayness of his hair. Dribble moved out of the corner of his mouth and he laughed, a coarse, unhappy sound.

"Daddy!"

The voice came from the darkened hallway beyond the open door. I turned, trying to see her, catching only the long white nakedness of her legs.

"Daddy," she said, "I told you not to come into this room. Please, Daddy."

The old man somehow pushed himself erect. His chest pouted out for one brief moment, then returned to its original position above his protruding stomach. He looked at the bottle, at me, at the sound of the voice; he mumbled something unintelligible and moved across the room, stumbling, making the doorway, disappearing.

She came through the doorway then, and I got to my feet. She was a little older than she appeared to be on the screen, but, still and all, she was positively the most shockingly beautiful woman I had even seen. The sunsuit was much too brief for my comfort.

"You must excuse Daddy, Mr. Phelan," she said. She paused. "You are Mr. Phelan?"

I nodded. The Filipino servant had let me in.

She sat down opposite me, crossing her legs. She seemed to fit in perfectly with the room, which was a strange mixture of period and modern. I noticed the beginnings of wrinkles of fat high on her thighs and felt embarrassed; I had found a flaw in what had been termed the perfect woman.

"I hope you don't think too ill of me, Mr. Phelan. Daddy is a hopeless lush. I tried, for some years, to have him cured. Several institutions, a lot of money." Her words came out in a sing-song manner, drifting over me. Her blue-gray eyes swept my face and she smiled. It was that famous smile. "Now," she went on, "I just let him drink. It's all he wants to do. It will kill him, eventually, but he'll die happy. I can't give him any more than that."

I said, "I'm not a nurse-maid for drunks, Miss Harding."

Someone laughed outside the house and I heard the distant splash of a body hitting water. Claire Harding gave me the benefit of a second smile.

"I hope that doesn't disturb you," she said. "Just some week-end guests. I don't swim myself, but my guests always enjoy the pool."

"That's understandable."

"You don't look like a private detective, Mr. Phelan. Horn-rimmed glasses, a moustache. Definitely not the Bogart type."

"I'm bigger than he is," I said.

She rose to her feet. "A drink?"

I thought of the old man. "No," I said.

"I didn't call you about Daddy, Mr. Phelan. I gave up

on him long ago. It's—" she paused, for the first time losing some of her regal air—"it's about another matter entirely. Quite an important matter."

"Importance is a matter of relativity, Miss Harding. What's important to you might not be so important to me."

She gave me a studied stare. "Come with me," she said. "I have something to show you. Or rather, someone."

I followed her across the room, and it was quite a hike. She paused at the wide, heavily curtained windows, standing back just far enough not to be visible from the outside. Her hand touched my arm, holding me.

I looked out through a small pencil of sunshine. There was a group of some ten or twelve people about a heart-shaped swimming pool. Two men with a lot of muscles and a lot of hair were in the water, bouncing a rubber ball back and forth between them. A stunningly beautiful brunette, very young and very appealing in a too-brief swim suit, stood on the diving board, her pose purposeful. She did a slow pivot, turning to walk off the diving board; she paused beautifully by the pool-side, then walked slowly across to sit beside a short, fat, bald-headed man.

"If that's what is troubling you," I said, "I can see your problem."

Claire Harding turned to look at me. Anger crossed her face and left it. She didn't like to be compared with other women, especially young ones.

"That, as you so aptly put it, Mr. Phelan, is not my problem. She's just a young slut. She has no talent."

"I could argue that point with you."

"Mr. Phelan—" her voice was caustic—"I don't want

to play word games with you. If you want this job, you'll please pay attention."

I felt properly reprimanded.

She turned back. "See that man?" she pointed with her hand and I sighted over the bright of her nails a broad-shouldered, dark-skinned man sitting beside the pool, his feet dangling in the water. "That's my problem."

The man's face was vaguely familiar to me. I tried to place it in my memory, but failed.

"That is my husband, Mr. Phelan. Harrison Woodward. You've undoubtedly heard of him?"

I placed him then. "Of course," I said.

"I thought so."

We made the long hike back across the room, resuming our sitting positions. She lit a cigarette, not offering me one. I would have enjoyed turning it down.

"Harrison is in some kind of trouble, Mr. Phelan," she said. "I'm not sure just what kind it is. But he hasn't been himself lately."

"You want me to find out what that trouble is?"

"That's right."

"Sounds simple enough."

"You come very highly recommended, Mr. Phelan. I've been told you're very discreet. I hope you can remain so."

"For fifty dollars a day," I said, "I can be the soul of discretion."

"I see." She laughed, suddenly, and with a good deal of force. "I once played in a private-eye movie, Mr. Phelan. It was years ago. I didn't think, then, that I would ever be consulting one in real life."

"Private eyes, as you call them, Miss Harding, are necessary evils."

"I guess they are."

I thought back to the last movie I had seen her in. She had been an Egyptian princess, or something like that; she was getting a little old for that type of role.

"Could it be woman trouble, Miss Harding?"

Again anger touched her face; this time it was replaced by an unnatural smile.

"Really, Mr. Phelan, let's not be naive. This is Hollywood, the land of the divorce. Marriages here are not quite as important as they are in—let's say, Sioux City. Harrison is my fourth husband. If he chooses to play around a little on the side, no harm is done."

"And you?"

The question seemed to startle her. She tapped a long finger against a naked knee. She moved the finger away; but I kept my eyes on the knee.

"My morals are my own, Mr. Phelan."

"I guess I am a little naive."

"I guess you are, at that."

"Then I'll rule out women, Miss Harding. What else remains?"

"That's why I'm going to pay you fifty dollars a day, Mr. Phelan."

I rose to my feet. She remained seated.

"I guess we understand each other," I said.

"I hope we do."

I, apparently, had been dismissed.

The old man was slumped in a chair by the outside door. His snores had an alcoholic tinge about them; the bottle lay at his feet, empty now.

The Filipino servant who had ushered me in now slipped silently out of a side door. He smiled knowingly at me, handing me a check. I thanked him, looking at the check. It was for $500.

I guessed she could afford it.

I parked in a lot near the Brown Derby at Hollywood and Vine. As I walked out of the lot, I noticed the theater marquee across the street—Claire Harding was starring in *Forever You*. Forever was a varying degree of time, depending on the woman—for Claire Harding, apparently, it was no time at all.

I had stopped at a gas station on the way in and called Jean MacNeece and she was waiting for me when I got out of the elevator on the third floor of the Vine Building. Jean was an old friend. Her face was too round and too freckled to be called pretty; she had the habit of looking at you with her head slightly cocked back, ready to throw her words at you. She worked for one of the trade papers. She did an occasional column on the happiness of various Hollywood marriages, but mostly she was an errand girl for the more widely known columnists.

"The poor woman's Sam Spade," she said by way of greeting.

I grunted at her. She was one of my favorite people, but why spoil your friends? I followed her through the clacking noise of the typewriters into the small cubicle that she called an office.

She sat down, propping her legs up on the corner of the desk before me, showing plenty of thigh. Her left stocking had a run in it an inch long.

"All right, Johnny boy," she said, "What'll it be? A little drink? A little sex?"

"Not today, honey. Business."

"Don't tell me you're working again?"

"That's right."

"You disappoint me, Johnny boy."

"I disappoint a lot of people. Mostly women."

The telephone rang. She looked at it disgustedly. It continued to ring. Finally she picked it up. "She's not here," she said. She replaced the telephone, looking at me, laughing a little.

"What do you know about Claire Harding?" I asked.

She straightened the skirt over her knees. Her eyes were serious.

"For the suckers, or you?"

"For me."

"She's a bitch."

I waited for her to continue.

"I mean that—you be careful. She's a first-class bitch. She's cut more throats in this business than I'd care to think about."

"She gave me a ten-day advance."

"That isn't all she'll give you if you stick around her. Believe me."

"How about her husband?"

"Harrison Woodward? Strictly a nothing, really a nothing. He made a couple of A's for MGM—or was it Warner's—and then folded completely. He does an occasional TV thing now, just for face. As the saying goes, he ain't got what it takes."

"He's in some kind of trouble. She wants me to bail him out."

"That figures."

"What kind of trouble, Jean? Any ideas?"

"With that guy it could be anything from booze to politics and picking the wrong horse or dame and back again. He's run the whole course."

The telephone rang again. She picked it up, said, "Yeah," and listened for a moment, jotting down something on a piece of scratch paper. She replaced the telephone.

"This is one helluva business, Johnny boy," she said. "Well, I've got to work. If I hear anything through the grapevine, I'll let you know."

I recognized the brush-off. I stood up, went to the door.

"Johnny boy," Jean said, "she's a bitch, believe me. Don't fall into the snake pit."

"I'm not her type."

"You're a man."

With that I left Jean MacNeece.

It was one of those hot and humid days. Smog banked against the hills above Hollywood Boulevard; tourists trotted along the street, their cameras vainly searching for a well-known face; newsboys half-heartedly yelled the latest news from Formosa; a pretty girl in a tight pink sweater waited through two green lights on the corner of Vine, making the day even warmer.

I went across the street to Mike Lyman's for a beer and a sandwich, then walked back to the parking lot.

I saw him sitting in my car and, as always, a bad taste came into my mouth. Jocko Quinn was not one of my favorite people. His fat little body was wedged into the front seat of my coupe. His mouth stretched into a wide grin, tightening the little red veins on his cheeks.

"My tried and true friend, John J. Phelan," he said.

"What in hell do you want, Jocko?"

"Is that any way to talk to me?"

I didn't answer him. I got in behind the wheel and filled a pipe. It was too hot to smoke it, so I put it aside. Jocko made a noise in the back of his throat. I held back my temper. Hitting him would be like sticking your fist into a bowl of raw liver.

"Let's take a ride," he said. "I got some talking to do."

"Not with me, you haven't."

The smile disappeared from his face and he puffed quickly on the stub of his cigar. The smoke and the smell combined to raise my temper and bring back memories. Jocko and I had teamed up on a few cases; it was something I wanted to forget.

"I'm busy, Jocko. Beat it!"

"With Claire Harding?"

I looked at him for a long moment, wondering how he knew my client's name.

"Don't try to kid me, Johnny," he said. "I got the straight dope and I got to talk to you. It's worth the effort."

Effort, with Jocko Quinn, was a valuable thing. He didn't like to move his fat little body unless it was absolutely necessary.

"For pete's sake," I said. "Throw away that cigar! It stinks to high heaven."

He assumed a hurt look, closed his eyes and opened them again. He took a last drag on the cigar, looked at it fondly, then dropped it out the window.

"What are you after, Jocko? What's your angle?"

His laugh was short. "You're a distrustful bastard, Johnny. I've got no angle, no angle at all. I just want to cut you in on something. Something big."

"Come on, come on, my time's valuable."

"Sure it is. I know that." The little fat hands moved across the big fat stomach. He took a deep sigh. "Let's take a ride."

"We can talk here."

He seemed to think that over. His head moved forward, trying to look out. We couldn't see the street from where we were parked. He was sweating and I was beginning to smell him; little rivers ran down his forehead, lining his face and features.

"Johnny," he said, "this is big. It's the biggest thing I've ever tried. I wouldn't cut you in, but—" his eyes searched my face for some sign of understanding—"but it's too big for me alone. You're the kind of guy that can handle it." He paused. The little fat hands moved again. "I tailed you from the Harding place."

"What were you doing out there?"

"Never mind that."

"I want to know."

"It's not important, Johnny."

I let that ride. The sun ricocheted off the windshield, stinging my eyes. I lit a cigarette. It was almost as bad as the pipe. Damn the heat.

"Believe me, Johnny, when I say this is big."

"Okay, so I believe you."

I didn't though. You couldn't believe Jocko Quinn, not and expect to know the truth.

He said, "A cool quarter-million bucks. Does that interest you, Johnny? Does it?"

I didn't answer. I watched a blonde climb into a Mercury convertible. She had nice legs.

"I can't handle it alone," he said. "Dammit, I wish I could! But I can't."

"You said that before."

"Yeah, so I did. Listen, Johnny, listen to me real close. I'm not bulling you. There's two hundred and fifty grand bouncing around here. Two hundred and fifty." The way he said the amount sent chills down my back.

"That's a lot of money. It's all tax-free, if we play our cards right."

"We?"

"Sure, Johnny. You and me. I'm going to cut you in. Just like old times, Johnny. We'll be working together again. Just like old times."

He was too nervous. The hands continued to move and he continued to sweat and the smell grew stronger.

"What's the pitch?"

"There's no pitch. This dough's just lying around, just waiting to be picked up."

It was a lot of money for a punk like Jocko Quinn to be worrying about; it was a lot of money for me, too. His eyes danced around in his face and I could see him forming the amount with his lips. I felt a little sick.

"You meet me tonight," he said. "Ten o'clock sharp. At Fairfax and Wiltshire."

"Why there? Why not my place?"

"I think I'm being tailed. I'm not sure."

"What's this got to do with Claire Harding?"

The little red veins tightened on his cheeks again.

"Not with her, Johnny, not with her."

"What were you doing out there?"

"I told you it wasn't important. Goddamn it, Johnny, do you want in on this or not?"

"All right," I said.

"You'll meet me tonight? Promise?"

I nodded.

I watched his little fat form waddle out of the parking lot. Jocko Quinn was getting in the big time. I still felt a little sick.

2

THE TELEPHONE WAS RINGING WHEN I
got to my apartment. I left the door open and picked up
the receiver.

"Hello," I said.

"Mr. Phelan?"

I recognized the voice.

"Yes."

"This is Claire—"

"I know."

A man and a woman walked by my open door. I heard
them laugh and then their footsteps going down the car-
peted stairs.

"No results yet," I said.

"Really, Mr. Phelan, I didn't expect any."

"Uh-huh. Miss Harding, do you know a Jocko Quinn?"

The telephone was silent. I tried to picture her in the
sunsuit—my watch said 5:30, though, and she was probably dressed by now.

"I don't think so," she said, after a while. "There was a
Jocko something-or-other in a picture I did about two
years ago. An Englishman, I think. A real bore, if I
remember correctly."

"Wrong man," I said.

18

She laughed suddenly, saying something to someone on her end of the line. I couldn't hear what she said, but I wished I could see her, see what was going on.

"Mr. Phelan," she said, "I'm having a little party tonight. Just a few friends. Perhaps you'd like to come?"

"In the line of duty?"

"In the line of duty."

I thought about it a moment.

"I'd be delighted."

"Fine. Around nine then, Mr. Phelan."

I thought of Jocko and the appointment.

"I'll be a little late. Maybe ten-thirty."

Her voice lost its pleasantness. "If that's the best you can do."

"It is. I'm a working man."

"You're working for me, aren't you?"

"That's right."

I could hear her fingers drumming against the receiver; the noise rebounded against my ears.

"No one need know about—"

"Of course not, Miss Harding."

"You are discreet, Mr. Phelan?"

"Always."

The telephone was dead, quite suddenly. She seemed to have a habit of ending things that way. I walked across the room, closing the door. The night promised to be a long one. I decided to catch forty winks.

The thing kept pushing at my shoulders. I tried to resist it, but it wouldn't go away. I opened my eyes. A face stood above me and a voice said something. The face was fuzzy. I reached over to the table by my bed, putting on my glasses.

The face took form and I recognized it. I swung up to a sitting position and recognized the other face, too. The faces belonged to Adam Wheeler, a detective-lieutenant in Homicide and a very intelligent cop, and to Hap Rossi, one step lower in rank and five steps lower in intelligence. Rossi was the one who had been pushing at me.

"Gents," I said, rising to my feet.

Wheeler didn't smile at me. He sat in a straight-backed chair by the window, cleaning his fingernails. Rossi glared at me from his tiny brown eyes—but, then, he always glared at me. He didn't like me and made no bones about it.

I walked into the kitchen, rinsed out a dirty glass, took a long drink of cold water, and came back into the other room.

"Been sleeping long, Johnny?" Wheeler asked.

I looked at the clock on the dresser. It said 8:20.

"Not long enough," I said.

"How long, Phelan?"

Rossi's bulk moved in front of me. His face was broad and dark and his head was rimmed with fuzzy black hair and quite bald in the middle. He was an ugly brute.

"Whoever gave you the name Hap?" I asked.

"Don't be a wise guy," he said.

His right hand tightened into a fist. He wouldn't need much to set him off.

I said, "Why all the build-up? What do you characters want?"

"How long, Johnny?"

I turned to Wheeler. "I don't know, Adam. I guess I lay down about five-thirty. Something like that."

"You sure, Phelan?" Rossi's face moved close to mine. He smelled of garlic. "You absolutely sure?"

I moved away from him, taking my pants from the back of a chair, putting them on. Rossi's huge hand dug into my shoulder, twisting me around. I slapped his hand away.

"Take it easy, Hap," said Wheeler.

"He ain't no friend of mine," said Rossi.

"Drop dead," I said.

"All right, all right, you two," said Wheeler. He rose to his feet, his frame casting a long shadow across the room.

"What in hell's going on here?" I asked.

"You tell us, wise guy," said Rossi.

Wheeler asked: "You own a fifty-two Dodge?"

"You know I do."

"Where is it?"

"The last time I saw it, it was parked right around the corner." I tried to smile. "It isn't hot, Adam."

"Cut the comedy," said Rossi.

"When's the last time you saw Jocko Quinn?"

I looked at Adam and he looked at me.

"Come on, Johnny," said Wheeler. "This is serious. When's the last time you saw him?"

I shrugged.

"This afternoon."

"What time this afternoon?"

"I don't know. I don't have the habit of timing my movements."

"Johnny," Wheeler's voice was tired.

"Just before I came home," I said. "Maybe four forty-five, maybe five o'clock. I'm not sure of the time."

"What did he want?"

I hesitated. Rossi began moving about the room, opening drawers, looking through them.

"What's that ape doing?" I asked.

"Cut it out, Hap," said Wheeler.

Rossi glared at both of us, but he stopped his search. "You didn't answer that last question, Johnny."

"I've got a client, Adam."

"And I've got a murder, Johnny."

It hit me. Two and two made four. Jocko Quinn had tried to play it too big. He had said he couldn't handle it alone. I wondered if whoever had been tailing him had seen him with me. I hoped not.

"Jocko Quinn?" I asked.

"That's right."

Rossi made guttural noises at me. Wheeler stared him down.

"Hap," he said, "you'd better check the rest of the neighborhood. See if anyone happened to see anything."

Rossi was unhappy with the assignment. He would much rather have played blood-in-the-gutter with me. He slammed the door on his way out.

I offered a cigarette to Wheeler. He shook his head. I lit my own.

"Why, Adam?"

"I was going to ask you that question."

I moved to the window. It was dark outside. A cat meowed and someone slammed a screen door. Tin cans fell against cement and the cat meowed again. I moved back to the middle of the room.

"You find him in my car?"

"Uh-huh. Two thirty-eight slugs in him. Looks like he was hit over the head first, then shot."

"I don't own a gun."

"I know that."

"How'd you find him?"

"A woman, walking along the street. He was lying half out of the car. She thought he was just a drunk. She opened the car door and he fell out. She screamed like bloody hell and some guy called us."

"Simple, isn't it?"

"I don't know, Johnny. Is it?"

I sat down on the bed. Wheeler scratched the back of his neck. We looked at each other.

I said: "You don't think—"

"You're not that dumb, Johnny."

"I hope to hell not."

"What did Jocko want this afternoon?"

I didn't answer.

"I thought you hated his guts."

"I do. I did. Everybody did."

"What did he want?"

I stared at him. He was a smart one. He'd been on the force for fifteen years. Nothing much slipped past this cop.

"I was working on a case," I said. "He had tailed me, wanted in on it. Apparently, things hadn't been too good for him lately. That's all."

I thought of the $250,000.

"Who's the client?"

"Can you sit on it?"

"I'm not promising you anything, Johnny. I've got a murder on my hands. Murder plays hell in the department. We've got to have a killer."

I said, "I'm not giving you a killer. I don't know that there's any connection. My client happens to be Claire Harding."

His face showed surprise. "The movie star?"

I nodded.

"Traveling big, Johnny? What does she need a goon like you for?"

"That's private, until you prove otherwise. Maybe she wanted to talk politics."

He mulled that over, then smiled, the first time he had done so.

"Okay, Johnny," he said, "that'll do. You haven't any idea why Jocko was killed?"

"Not one, Adam."

Lying comes easy in this business.

"You'll be around?"

"Of course. I'm going out to the Harding place to-night."

"Business or pleasure?"

I smiled now. "Business."

His smile broadened. "I've heard of her. Need any help?"

"You're married."

"Uh-huh," he said. He moved to the door, pausing with his hand on the knob. "You can't use your car. It's impounded."

"Thanks."

"If you happen to think of anything, any reason for Jocko being killed, you'll let me know?"

"I can give you a thousand reasons," I said. "For one thing, he smelled in hot weather."

Wheeler nodded, seriously. "Dead or alive." He added: "I'd hate to think you've been lying to me, Johnny. I like you."

"It's mutual."

He left.

I took off my pants and went into the shower. The water stung my head, trying to beat some sense into it. I wondered just where that $250,000 Jocko had talked about was. I could use it. The thought of the Riviera came to me again.

3

THE CABBIE SWORE LOUDLY AT THE Cadillac convertible which had swerved in front of us. We turned off Sunset, going north. The houses were in the six-figure bracket, though you couldn't see them; they were well hidden behind trees and a varying type of high wall; occasional lights sprinkled the dark night and I tried not to think of Jocko Quinn. The cab cut sharply into a driveway, slowing between a host of Cadillacs and Jaguars. I was out of my class, way out.

The door opened before I had a chance to ring the bell. The Filipino's smile was automatic as I handed him my hat. He motioned me towards the front room and the smile disappeared.

It was a small affair, at that. Thirty or forty people lounged about in the gigantic room, all of them seemingly talking at once; smoke clung to the ceiling, drifting above their heads. I could hear another group out by the pool.

No one paid any attention to me. I looked for either Claire Harding or her husband, seeing neither. I did see the young brunette who had modeled the bikini at the pool that morning. She was the central interest of four men, all of them talking only to her, all of them bald, all of them old enough to be her father, or maybe even grandfather. She was dressed in a white knitted suit with a turtle-neck, and there was no room for improvement. Her eyes caught mine, paused on my face for a moment trying to recognize me, then passed on. I could do her no good.

I elbowed my way through the room. Claire Harding was by the pool. She was dressed in an off-the-shoulder black thing that did much for her. She was talking to two women and a man. The man walked away, looking as if he were angry about something. She followed him amusedly with her eyes, then caught sight of me. Her right hand came out in a signal and the two women turned to look at me.

I made it to her side. She gave me a smile.

"Mr. Phelan," she said, "so good of you to come."

I smiled my thanks at her courtesy. I suddenly found myself wondering where Daddy was. Did she hide him at these gatherings?

I caught the tail-end of her introduction.

". . . is a writer. Really a good one, too, you know. Surely you've read some of his things."

One of the women stared at me. She had tight blonde hair that should have been gray by now, a prominent nose and far too much makeup.

"I do so love writers," she said.

I played along. " So do I."

Claire Harding was having her moment. The corners of her mouth twitched. "What was the name of your last book, Mr. Phelan?"

"*Mind Over Mayhem*," I said.   "Claire, dear."

Her eyebrows rose and then fell again. She had approved of me.

"And quite an exciting book, too," said Claire Harding.

"No complaints yet," I said.

Someone's scream pierced the night behind me. I turned just in time to see two men throw a young girl, fully clothed, into the pool. Her body splashed into the water and waves bumped against the side of the pool and then she bobbed to the surface, swearing at everyone. One of the men jumped in beside her and everyone laughed. Everyone but me.

Claire Harding touched my arm and I followed her through the laughing idiots to a halfway secluded place near the back of the house. We stood on the edge of a ring of colored lights which surrounded the pool. The faint scent of pine touched my nostrils.

"Nice friends you have," I said.

"They'll do. You caught my cue nicely, Mr. Phelan. You look like a writer. I hope you didn't mind."

"For fifty dollars a day," I said, "you can make believe I'm anything you want."

"Anything?"

I nodded.

"You're taking a chance, Mr. Phelan."

"Is your husband here?" I might as well work a little, I thought.

"Yes. Somewhere. I'm not just sure where."

"I'll find him."

"I imagine you will, Mr. Phelan."

She waved her hand, dismissing me. I was replaced by two young men with wavy black hair and muscles.

The girl had been following my movements for some time. Finally I turned, raising my glass in a mock salute to her. She returned the gesture, walking towards me. Her face just missed being beautiful; it was wide, with high cheekbones and an overly large mouth. Her bright black hair was cut short, her legs were long and trim and her bosom was quite ample, even in this crowd.

"You should have punted on fourth down, Mr. Phelan." Her smile was quick, but warm.

"I don't get you."

"You're caught in your own territory."

I shrugged.

"Harrison Woodward left almost an hour ago."

"I don't—"

"Mr. Phelan—" the smile maintained its warmth—"I'm Dianne Cochran, Miss Harding's personal secretary. I might even go farther than that. I'm also her confidante."

"That's how you knew me?"

She nodded. "That's how."

A waiter came by with a tray of fresh drinks. We helped ourselves. It wasn't often I got a chance at such good stuff.

"It looks like I goofed," I said.

"Could be," she said. "You could stand in line for that, though."

"You talk in circles, Miss Cochran."

"Dianne will do, John."

"All right, Dianne. You still talk in circles."

"Part of my charm."

She had charm all right. Enough to interest me.

A handsome young thing wearing a bright new mustache swayed by. He smiled at the girl by my side. She turned her head.

"Some of these jokers make me sick," she said. There was unhidden disgust in her eyes and I didn't feel so alone any more. The odds had been cut down. There were two of us now.

A sudden hush fell over the room. The young brunette with all the equipment was standing on a table in the middle of the room. She had removed the white knitted suit; as a matter of fact, she had removed almost everything that counted. Someone began playing a piano in a slow, blue-sy way. The girl's tanned body began swaying slowly in a wide circle, keeping time with the music. A man coughed to my left and a woman suppressed a giggle. Dianne said something under her breath; I didn't catch it. I could see the perspiration on the back of the neck of the man in front of me. It brought back the picture of Jocko Quinn and I erased that with another look at the brunette. Suddenly a little man with thick glasses jumped up on the table beside her and they both fell off into a welter of people.

Noises slowly returned to the room. I felt quite warm. It was some party.

"There'll be more entertainment later on," said Dianne. Her voice was as dry as a desert breeze.

"Such as?"

"Such as movies. The kind that most of these damned idiots like."

The look she gave me was unkind.

"You don't?"

"Mr. Phelan," she said, "I am a normal woman. I like the opposite sex. I like it very much. It's a great invention and I've had my fun during my 24 years. But I don't go for some of the things they hand out around here."

"You could quit."

She only looked at me, then turned away. I watched her walk through the maze of people. She stopped at the entrance to a hallway, turning to look at me, her hand resting lightly on the wall. Her fingers fluttered at me and then she was gone.

I listened to the talk going on; it bounced off me like so much nothing. I took her route through the crowd and entered the hallway. It was dark, lighted only by a single blue bulb from the far end. I walked along the hallway slowly. At a partly open door I heard soft music. A girl sighed, a young sound.

The girl's voice, young, tinny, said, "You sure about this, Eddie?"

A man's voice replied, "Would I kid you, honey-baby, would I?"

"I've got to be sure."

"Honey-baby."

The girl sighed again.

I put my hand on the door, then hesitated. To hell with it, I thought. This house was a jungle and animals will be animals.

I moved on down the hallway, stopping at the next door. The room beyond it was dark. I reached in, switched on the light. Dianne sat in a huge leather chair by wide French doors. She looked at me.

"Sex," she said.

"Yeah," I said. "It comes and it goes."

"It only comes around this house," she said. She curled her long legs beneath her, settling more firmly in the chair. There was a vague familiarity about her, something I couldn't place.

The room, apparently, was the library. Three walls were lined with books, hiding behind glass cases. The books were unused.

"They came with the house?" I asked.

She grinned. "Let's be friends."

I moved over to the chair, sat on its arm. I leaned down, tipped her chin up, kissed her on the mouth; her mouth moved under mine, her fingers dug into the back of my neck—then she pushed me away.

"No," she said. "Not here. Not in this house."

"Any time, any place," I said.

She looked up at me and I moved away. She lit two cigarettes, giving me one, and we watched the clouds of smoke form and disappear.

"What did you mean out there?" I asked. "About the line."

Her eyes hovered uncertainly on mine. "A kiss and then a question. Is that the way you work?"

"The kiss was for free," I said.

She looked at the tip of her cigarette and shrugged. "You're the third detective Claire has hired to find out about Harrison."

An idea struck me head-on. I didn't like it. "Was Jocko Quinn one of them?"

"You asked Claire that this afternoon."

"I'm asking you now."

"Yes," she said. "He was the second one."

"Dianne," I said, "friend Jocko is no longer with us. Someone put two thirty-eight slugs in him this evening and left his body in my car."

There was nothing on her face. Nothing.

"Who was the first one, Dianne?"

"A Harry Dexter," she said, "A poor little man. He was killed in an auto accident."

I could have kicked myself all the way to Hollywood and Vine. A hundred ideas flashed across my mind and all of them melted down to this—I was a pigeon.

"You talk too much, Dianne!"

I turned around. Claire Harding stood in the doorway. Her face was flushed, whether from drink or from something else I didn't know.

"Look, baby," I said, "I don't like you."

A smile touched her lips. "That's understandable," she said. "Not many people do."

"You could have told me about these other two guys."

She shrugged.

"I'll mail you your check."

"You're quitting?"

"Naturally."

She walked across the room, stopping before Dianne. She touched the younger girl's head affectionately; she was nearer to being a human being at that moment than at any other time I had seen her.

"Have it your way, Mr. Phelan," she said.

"I will."

I left the room and the house.

4

I OPENED THE DOOR TO MY OFFICE,
stooped down to pick up the morning mail. The first
three envelopes held bills. The fourth envelope interested me. It was small and my name and address were
scrawled across it in a childish hand. The writing belonged to Jocko Quinn. I opened the envelope and a key
fell out on the desk. There was nothing else. The key
was the kind used for rental boxes in bus and train
stations. The number on it was 3752. I started to dial
the Hollywood bus terminal.

"Good morning."

I looked up. Dianne Cochran stood in the doorway.
She looked fresh and animated—curiously better than
she had last night, in that house. Her blue suit was expensive and in good taste.

I searched through my wallet for the check, found it.
I put it on the desk.

"Is this what you came for?"

She shook her head. "No. May I sit down?"

I shrugged. She moved into the chair opposite me.

"You're a hard man, Mr. Phelan."

"Just an act, for my customers' benefit."

"I guessed as much."

"Okay," I said, "let's have it."

"Have what?"

"Whatever it's going to be. The pitch. I've heard them all in this business."

"There's no pitch, Mr. Phelan," she said. "We need your help. It's that simple."

"We?"

"Yes. Mother and I."

That stunned me. I looked at her. There *was* a resemblance—I had noticed it the night before, but had not added it up.

"Don't be embarrassed, Mr. Phelan. I'm not."

"Why should I be embarrassed?"

"Most people are, when they find out. You see, I was born out of wedlock. There's a name for people like me, but I don't like to use it."

"I don't blame you."

She seemed to think that over.

"People make mistakes," I said.

She nodded. "Mother was only 17. She didn't know any better."

That was one way to put it. I said, "I understand."

But I didn't. Just why she should be telling me this, I didn't know. I wasn't sure that I wanted to know, either.

The telephone rang. I was thankful for that.

It was my answering service. A Mr. Carter had called. He would be a little late in paying his bill. I had tailed his wife for a week. She hadn't done anything wrong— apparently Mr. Carter wasn't happy about it. I hung up the phone.

"We're willing to raise the fee, Mr. Phelan—to twenty-five hundred.

Twenty-five hundred wouldn't take me to the Riviera, but it could mean Mexico City for a few weeks. I took out a scratch pad and a pencil and began doodling. I made a large circle, then a smaller one; I put a nose on the smaller one, then ears on the outer one. She smiled.

"That's a bad habit," she said.

"All habits are bad," I said.

She held out a cigarette. I didn't move. She frowned at me, lighting it herself.

I pulled out a pipe, filled it, lit it. My clouds were bigger than hers. That didn't give me any satisfaction.

"Miss Cochran," I said.

"It was Dianne last night. That'll do this morning, too."

I said, "A jinx seems to go with this job. Jocko Quinn worked for Miss Harding, for you. They found him dead in my car. I knew this other man slightly, this Harry Dexter. As you said, he was a nice little man; he never harmed anyone. Maybe he was killed in an auto accident, maybe he wasn't. I remember reading about it in the papers. I even sent flowers to his funeral. But I'm no hero, not at all. I did enough of that kind of fighting in the war, enough to last me a lifetime."

"Maybe the other two weren't smart enough."

"Maybe they weren't. Maybe I'm no smarter."

"I doubt that."

"Doubt it if you want. It's my life."

She stubbed her cigarette out in an ashtray, then rearranged herself in the chair. She played with the red leather purse in her lap and her eyes moved across my face.

"I told Claire you wouldn't do it."

"You were right."

"No harm in asking."

"None."

"Five thousand?"

The thought of the Riviera returned. Nice young things in next-to-nothing bathing suits; pleasant Mediterranean breezes; long, cool nights to do nothing; Monte Carlo.

"On two conditions," I said suddenly. "I want the money in advance. And you don't play games with me. I want facts, all of them you can give me. I've got two strikes on me at the start. I don't want to strike out."

She put a lot into her smile, opened her purse, handed me an envelope. I opened it. It held a check payable to John J. Phelan. The amount was $5,000. I looked at her and we both laughed.

We drove out Sunset in her MG. She was an excellent driver. I had the idea that she would be good at anything she tried. Claire Harding was to meet us at a cabin at Malibu.

We came out on the Coast Highway, turning north, toward Malibu. The ocean was quiet, disturbed only by a slow-moving tanker; early morning fog still clung to the distant horizon. She parked on the shoulder of the highway and I followed her down a narrow path. The cabin was small and dirty on the outside, battered by years of salt air and ocean winds. We disturbed a flock of sea gulls and they flew off.

The cabin had two rooms—a combination sleeping-and-living room and a kitchen. The furniture was expensive and in good taste. I opened the french doors fronting to the water and took in a lungful of salt air.

Dianne shrugged out of her suit coat, revealing a sleeveless white blouse. Her arms were long and deeply tanned. She looked at her watch.

"Claire won't be here until one," she said. "How about some chow?"

I agreed. I heard her busying herself in the kitchen and sat down in a deep leather chair, stretched my legs before me. I filled and lit a pipe, feeling very domestic. It was a pleasant morning. I watched the gentle movement of the ocean; a motorboat skimmed by, turned at a sharp angle, sending white puffs of water in all directions, and then disappeared. A dog barked. I moved out of the chair, going to the telephone. I wasn't being paid to dream. I dialed the downtown police station, asking for Adam Wheeler.

"Adam?"

"Yes. Johnny?"

"That's right. Anything new?"

"What would be new?"

"I don't know. You're the cop."

A chuckle drifted across the wire. "I can't figure a thing, Johnny," he said. "Not one damned thing. Did you know Quinn had worked for your client?"

"I found it out. Last night."

"You sure?"

"I wouldn't lie to you, Adam."

"I hope not."

"Adam, do you remember Harry Dexter?"

"A tiny little guy, about the size of a jockey?"

"That's right."

"Uh-huh. I remember him. Killed in an auto accident a couple months ago."

"Anything fishy about that accident?"

There was silence. Dianne smiled out at me from the kitchen. I felt something flip within me.

"Why, Johnny?"

"No reason. Just thought I'd ask."

"I'll check it."

"Fine. Can I have my car back?"

"Not yet, Johnny. Don't get impatient."

"How's that ape you work with?"

"Rossi?"

"Yeah."

"He still hates your guts."

"Give him my love."

I hung up.

Dianne came out with a tray of hamburgers and two cold beers. I took a sip of the beer, and then ate two hamburgers and then finished the beer. I watched her carry the tray and the two empty glasses back into the kitchen and wondered if she would like the Riviera. A guy gets funny ideas sometimes.

"Tell me about him," I said.

"Who?"

She held out a cigarette and this time I lit it; she gave me a small, victorious smile.

"Your stepfather."

"Harrison?" She laughed. "I don't think of him as my stepfather. As a matter of fact, I hardly think of him at all. I think Claire is making a lot out of nothing."

"Then why did you come to my office this morning?"

"She asked me to."

"Do you get along with him?"

"As well as could be expected, I guess. We're on speaking terms."

"What kind of trouble could he be in?"

The long, tanned arms rose and fell in the air.

"I told you I wanted facts," I said. "I don't want to play games with you. If I'm going to find out about this guy, I've got to have a little more cooperation from the home team."

She rose, walked about the room. She flipped the cigarette out the door and looked at her watch.

"Hiring a private detective wasn't my idea, John," she said. "I don't intend to be grilled by you about either my mother or Harrison Woodward."

"In other words, you won't cooperate?"

"It's not that simple."

"How simple is it?"

"Cut it out, John."

Her face hid behind a calm mask. I rose, strode over to her. The smell of the perfume grew stronger. I put my hand out, caught her behind the neck, pulling her close to me. She resisted.

"No more of that," she said.

She looked at her watch again and this time I looked at mine. The time was 1:40. She went to the telephone, calling the Harding house. She hung up the receiver, turning to me.

"I'm worried, John," she said. "Claire left the house at eleven forty-five. She should have been here by now."

She began pacing back and forth. She called the house again; Miss Harding had not returned.

I had smoked three pipes before Claire Harding finally showed up. She opened the door, standing just inside it like a little girl caught stealing something. She tried to smile, but it didn't come off. There was an ugly bruise below her left eye and the blood had dried into cakes on her lips. She poked at her mussed hair with tender fingers and looked at me.

There was hate in her eyes, hate enough for the whole world.

5

CLAIRE HARDING SAT ON THE COUCH. She tried to smoke a cigarette through her puffed lips, but it was no go. She looked at the cigarette disgustedly, stubbing it out in an ashtray.

"Thank God I'm not in a picture now," she said. "I must look a mess."

My admiration for her was growing.

"Did Harrison do this, Mother? Did he?"

Claire Harding looked up at her daughter. She said, "It's the last time that sonofabitch will ever touch me." Anger and hate played with her eyes. "I could kill him."

"Take it easy," I said. "There are two dead men now. Don't go making rash statements. They might bounce on you."

"I don't give a damn," she said.

I had the feeling she didn't, either. She was a woman who would play what she started to the end, regardless of the consequences.

Claire's eyes clouded and I heard a movement behind me. I turned, seeing the guy close the door behind him. He smiled at us each in turn, but the .38 automatic he held in his right hand pointed only at me.

"Greetings," he said.

He was medium-sized, thin through the shoulders, with baggy eyes and a round, pixie-like face. I moved slightly, and the three eyes followed me, his two and the eye of the .38. My gaze traced along the dark blue barrel to his hand, and then I thought he was awfully dumb— the safety was on. I decided to play along with him.

"What are you doing here?" he asked me.

"I don't think that's any of your business."

The gun muzzle shifted, settling on a point in my midsection.

"Don't get tough," he said.

"Go to hell," I said.

His round face lost its confidence and he stepped back, leaning against the closed door. He pulled a cigarette out of his coat pocket, stuck it in his mouth, thumbed a wooden match to flame. The smoke hid his face for a moment, then he reappeared.

"You're a dumb bastard," I said.

The smile was small and hard. "You've seen too many movies, tough guy," he said.

"Enough," I said. I looked at the two women. Claire sat quite still on the couch; Dianne hovered in the background, her eyes on the gun. "Either of you know this guy?" They both shook their heads. I looked back at him. "That's a nice gun. A guy I know was killed with a thirty-eight, just last night."

The shock was genuine on his face. He frowned and took two quick puffs on the cigarette, then dropped it to the floor, grounding it out with the heel of his shoe.

"Okay," he said, "we've talked it enough."

"I think so, too," I said.

I moved across the room, toward him. He lifted the gun, pointing it at my head. I doubt he would have had the guts to pull the trigger regardless of the safety. I slapped the gun aside and then slapped his face. He dropped the gun and crawled along the wall. I caught him by the neck of his silk sports shirt and banged him against the wall. I hit him once, in the stomach, and he folded over, dropping to his knees. I stooped over, picking up the .38 automatic. I looked at it for a moment, then stuck it in my coat pocket.

I turned back to the two women. Claire gave me a wide smile; Dianne didn't give me anything.

"You two run along," I said. "I'll follow shortly. I want to talk to this guy."

They did as I said.

He sat up, leaning his back against the wall of the cabin. He looked at me once and then away again.

I asked, "Who are you?"

He didn't answer.

I walked over to him, lifted him to his feet. He punched me half-heartedly in the stomach and I backhanded him. A thin trickle of blood spoiled his lips. I turned him around, face to the wall, and searched him. He carried three one-dollar bills, a comb, a key ring with four keys on it, and sixty-three cents in loose change. He also had two dirty white handkerchiefs and a wallet without money, but with a snapshot of a chubby girl in a swimming suit, three business cards and a loose piece of scratch paper. The first card read, JIMMIE WARING, PRIVATE INVESTIGATOR, the second, HAROLD G. THOMPSON. The third card was the same as the first. I unfolded the piece of scratch paper. On the inside someone had written in pencil the telephone number, HO 4-9921, and the name, Sally. I looked up at him again.

"Okay," I said, "talk."

He grunted at me.

I took his .38 out of my pocket, clicked off the safety. I aimed it out at the ocean and fired it through the open door. The sound shocked the stillness. I looked back at him. He bit at his lower lip. I brought the .38 around, pausing with it on his face. He began to sweat.

"Don't get nervous," I said. "Just talk. Tell me all about it."

"I guess I'm not so good at this," he said.

I agreed with him, silently.

He took another cigarette out of his pocket. His hands were shaking and it took him two matches to light it. He inhaled deeply and then moved away from the wall, sitting in a chair. He slumped way down. He sniffled and wiped his nose with the back of his hand.

"This isn't getting us any place," I said.

I put the safety back on and dropped the gun in my pocket. He looked relieved.

"A guy hired me to tail the Harding dame," he said. He didn't look at me when he said it.

"You'll have to do better than that."

"It's the truth. So help me."

"What guy?"

"Just a guy."

"I want names."

He hesitated. "Harold G. Thompson," he said.

"Then you're Waring?"

He nodded.

"How long you been tailing her?"

"Since this morning."

"Tell me about it."

Again he hesitated. I moved to my feet, crossed the room and heard his feet shuffling softly against the carpet. I turned. He was about six feet away from me.

"I've got two inches and forty pounds on you," I said.

"I'm not much good with these anyway," he said. He looked down at his hands. "Christ," he said.

"Tell me about it," I said again. "All about it."

"This Thompson hired me to tail her, that's all," he said. "He came into my office this morning, gave me a week's advance, and gave me her description and house number. Christ, I didn't need her description. I've seen her in enough movies." His eyes wandered around the room. "I went out to her house and sat in my car. She came out—"

I interrupted: "What time?"

"Just before noon. About that time."

Maybe he was telling the truth. He was dumb enough to be capable of anything.

"Go on."

"I tailed her to an apartment in Santa Monica. She stayed in there for a couple of hours and when she came out, she was all beat up. You saw her. But I didn't butt in, not me. She came straight from there to here."

"How come you came in here with the gun?"

He lit another cigarette. His hands were calmer.

"I figured on a heist," he said. "Christ, I needed the dough. I'm in debt up to my fanny."

"Brother," I said, "you'll be in debt all your life."

"You going to call the cops?"

"What would you do?"

"I'd be big-hearted about it. I haven't any record. I wouldn't like to start now."

I laughed at him. A million little guys had a million different little excuses for doing what they did.

"Who is Thompson?" I asked.

"I don't know," he said. "He just came in my office. Like I said, he gave me a week's advance. He said he was a writer. He gave me that card and I put it in my wallet. I don't know where he lives, or anything about him. He paid cash. I didn't argue with him. I need the money."

"What was the address of the apartment in Santa Monica?"

"Seven-oh-nine Crescent Way. I don't know which apartment she went in, though. There're six of them."

"Okay, Junior," I said. "Beat it."

He looked at me with gratitude. "I'll remember this," he said. "Thanks."

"Go to hell," I said.

He all but ran out and I went to the telephone, dialing my answering service. Adam Wheeler had called twice. I dialed his number. He answered the phone and we exchanged pleasantries.

"Johnny," he said, "what made you ask about Dexter?"

"Just a hunch."

"Let me in on it."

"I can't, Adam. Not now. What about him?"

"He was drunk." He hesitated. "There were no witnesses. He was found in his car out on Pico. He had run into an embankment."

"Thanks, Adam," I said.

"Johnny, what's going on?"

"Sorry, Adam."

I hung up. Then, I called a cab. After that, I dialed

another number. I got hold of Mannie Mendosa. Mannie was a part-time welterweight who did odd jobs for me. I gave him Harrison Woodward's description and the number of the Harding house. I told him to hang around out there; if he caught sight of Woodward, Mannie was to tail him.

6

THE CAB LET ME OUT AT A U-DRIVE
place on Sunset. I rented a '51 Plymouth sedan and
started out for the evening. I had two stops to make.
The first was at a walk-up apartment in the low-rent
district near MacArthur Park.

I rang the bell and a little girl answered the door.

"Is your mother in?"

She stared up at me, then suddenly darted off. Her
place was taken by a small woman with fattish arms and
dull gray eyes.

"Mrs. Dexter?" I asked.

She nodded.

"I'm John J. Phelan, Mrs. Dexter. I was a friend of
your husband's."

"He didn't have any friends."

I let that pass. She played with the door knob.

"He's dead," she cried.

· "I know that."

A baby began to cry somewhere in the back of the
apartment. Mrs. Dexter turned, looking in the direction
of the noise. She shrugged her shoulders and gave me
a weary stare.

"I'd like to talk to you, Mrs. Dexter."

"I'm busy," she said. "What you got to talk about?"

49

"Your husband," I said.

The baby continued to cry. She scratched at the heavy brown rag that passed for her hair. She opened the door farther, allowing me to come in. We walked into the room that smelled of sour milk and unclean bodies. A table in one corner was filled with dirty dishes and two tin cans added their dignity to the floor. An old mohair chair matched its three holes with those of an equally old mohair couch.

The little girl came out. She looked at Mrs. Dexter.

"Mummy, Mummy," she said, "he's all wet."

Her eyes were wide with excitement. She had made a discovery.

"He's always wet, that one." Mrs. Dexter's voice was tired and beat. The baby's crying hung in the air. "Change him, Sylvia." She hesitated. "Please."

Sylvia dashed away, happy with her assignment. The baby's cries gradually dissipated into a gurgle and then into silence. The silence was crushing. Mrs. Dexter sat down on the couch, avoiding the holes. She crossed her legs; they were full of varicose veins.

"All right, Mr. Phelan," she said. "What is it?"

"I don't like to do this, Mrs. Dexter."

"The hell you don't. You wanted to talk—now, talk."

I chose a straight-back chair. Its legs were not too steady.

"I'd offer you a drink, Mr. Phelan," she said, "but I can't afford it any more. Not and buy milk for that baby. Harry didn't leave me a dime, not one damned dime."

She began to irritate me. I remembered Harry Dexter. He had been a quiet little man with a dogged persistency about him. I studied a fingernail.

"He's been dead almost nine weeks," she said. "It's been hard on me. Awfully hard."

"He was killed in an auto accident?"

"You know that. Why ask me?"

It was a good question. I shrugged.

I said, "I understand that the traffic report showed he had been drinking."

"The report was wrong. Harry never touched a drop." She laughed, showing a mouth full of even white teeth: they didn't fit with the rest of her appearance. "I was the drinking member of this family, not Harry."

"Did you tell that to the police?"

"Of course. What the hell did you expect me to do?"

The little girl showed up again. "He's changed, Mummy," she said.

Mrs. Dexter didn't look at her. "You go to bed, Sylvia."

Sylvia gave me a quick smile and I smiled back. She vanished.

"That's a nice little girl," I said.

"Don't make small talk, Phelan," she said. "You want something. Get to the point."

"I'm not sure your husband's death was accidental."

Her eyes wrinkled again and she scratched at the heavy brown rag. Her mouth opened and shut again.

"What do you want, mister? Do you want me to agree with you, is that what you want? All right, I do. It wasn't an accident."

"Did you tell that to the police?"

She shrugged. "Why bother? What good would it have done me? Harry was already dead. I loved him once—" her eyes drifted back through time— "about ten years ago. Things were different then. Love isn't enough. You need a little something else, too. I don't know what the hell that something is, but you need it."

"Neither do I, Mrs. Dexter."

I got to my feet. Coming here had been like a quick trip into a barrel of bad dreams. Mrs. Dexter crossed her hands in her lap, looking down at them. Her hands were red and brittle-looking.

"They were pretty once," she said.

"Yeah," I said.

She looked up at me. "You and Harry were friends?"

I nodded.

"The poor bastard," she said. "He was such a poor bastard. He couldn't do nothing right. Nothing."

I moved to the door.

"You couldn't spare a few bucks for an old friend's widow, could you?"

The smile was like the face behind it, dead, but not buried. I took a ten from my wallet and put it on a table. She spread her nostrils in appreciation.

As I closed the door behind me, I heard the baby start to cry again. Maybe Harry Dexter wasn't so badly off, after all.

My second stop was at my office. I parked a block away on Hollywood Boulevard, cut across the street. A kid in a pork-pie hat and an old Ford convertible almost ran me down. His unkind words about my antecedents followed me into the building. A form moved out of the darkness, and I felt for the .38 in my pocket.

"Okay, Johnny."

It was Adam Wheeler. He was alone.

"Hello, Adam."

"Let's go upstairs."

We went up to my office. I clicked on the light. The place was as it usually was. Wheeler began the ritual of cleaning his fingernails, a habit he had when disturbed about something.

"I don't think you're playing kosher with me, Johnny," he said.

I raised my right hand and smiled. "Honest Injun."

He didn't smile. He continued the work on the nails.

I walked around the desk. The key was still there. Like an idiot, I had left it right on top of the desk. I picked it up, slipping it into my pocket.

"We can't pick up a damn thing on Jocko Quinn," Adam said. "He had been working for Claire Harding, but quit." He looked at me carefully. "It was a clean job. He was sapped and then shot. The department is stumped. That make you happy, Johnny?"

"Come off it, Adam."

He put the finishing touches on a nail, folded the clippers up neatly, and put them away.

"Every guy that ever knew Quinn had a reason to kill him," I said. "He just plain stunk. You know why I split with him six months ago. Blackmail. The dirty kind. His was a filthy little perverted mind, Adam. I didn't like him. I'm sorry that he's dead."

"That's putting it on the line."

"Why not?" I asked.

"He was found in your car, Johnny. The people downtown want to know about that. I want to know about it." He moved into the center of the room. A light blinked on and off from a neon sign across the street. His face changed from white to red, white to red. "I could pick you up, Johnny."

"Don't kid me."

"I'm not kidding you."

I knew he wasn't. Just why I was keeping anything at all a secret from him, I wasn't sure. Maybe it was the $250,000.

"Rossi makes a good case against you. He says you're smart enough to have killed Quinn and then dumped him in your own car, just to throw us off. That would be smart, Johnny. It's been done before. You've got a reputation for being a smart guy. No one would think you dumb enough to put the body in your own car."

"You're talking through your hat."

"I know I am. Rossi doesn't."

"He doesn't like me. He wants to get me."

Wheeler moved away from the blinking light. "Johnny," he said, "I like you. I'd like you whether we'd been together in the war or not. My wife likes you and my two kids like you. But that won't stop me, Johnny, if you turn out to be a foul ball."

"Believe me, I won't."

"I'd like to believe you."

He removed his hat and ran his fingers through his thinning dark hair, then replaced the hat.

"Dexter worked for the Harding dame, too."

I shrugged.

"How come you were suspicious about him?"

"I thought it might add up."

"Does it, Johnny?"

"I don't know. Not yet. I can't tie it in yet."

I put my hand in my coat pocket. The .38 was still there. I brought it out and dumped it on the desk.

"That's how smart I am," I said. "There's a gun that might possibly have killed Quinn. It's got my prints all over it."

He looked at me and then at the gun. He put a pencil through the trigger guard, lifting the gun to his nose, smelling it.

"Who'd you shoot recently?"

"Target practice," I said.

"Where'd you get it?"

"I found it."

"God damn you, Johnny!"

His face was angry now. He leaned across the desk, and his mouth set in a hard straight line. He wasn't friendly any more: he was a cop, doing his job.

"I took it off a guy this afternoon," I said. "A funny little guy with a funny little face. He tried to hold me up."

"And you took it away from him? Just like that?"

"Just like that. It was simple. His name is Jimmie Waring and he claims to be a private dick. He was tailing my client and got a little too close."

Wheeler's mouth softened somewhat.

"One of these days, Johnny," he said, "you're going to get too smart."

I smiled at him.

"I wouldn't have given the gun to you if I actually thought it was the one. It'll give you something to do."

"I haven't got enough to do," he said. He scratched at his cheek. He needed a shave and he looked tired. "Sometimes I think every two-bit hood in the country comes to L.A. just to bother me."

I was glad I wasn't a cop.

"I'll check the gun," he said.

"Just in case," I said. "I've got two witnesses that saw me take it away from this Waring."

"They won't believe this downtown," he said.

"You're in so solid down there, they'd believe anything you said."

He looked at me quietly. He dug in his pocket and came out with a piece of gum. He folded the gum in half and put it in his mouth; his jaws moved slowly.

"You know, Johnny," he said, "my old man was a cop. He was a cop for twenty-two years and then some cheap hood knifed him in the gut. The old man didn't want me to be a cop. I don't know what he wanted me to be, but it wasn't a cop. He used to sit there, night after night, and tell me about it. The people don't appreciate cops, he would say. Damned if I don't believe him."

"There are cops and cops," I said. "And there are people and people."

He gave me a long look and then turned, walked out. I leaned back in the chair and thought about Adam Wheeler. He was a damned good cop; they didn't come any better. He was also a damned good man.

I gave him ten minutes and then went out myself. I walked to the Hollywood bus terminal, searched the rental boxes until I found the one with the number matching the key. Jocko Quinn had been lazy; I had figured that he would take the nearest station. My hands shook a little as I put the key in the slot and opened the box. There was a small envelope inside, and I felt disappointed. It was too small to contain $250,000.

I opened the envelope; it held a piece of lined paper. The printing was in Jocko's childish hand. I read:

JOHNNY: IF YOU GET THIS, I WON'T BE ALIVE. THIS IS A BIG THING, THE BIGGEST THING I HAVE EVER TRIED. IT WAS TOO BIG FOR HARRY DEXTER. I

MAILED YOU THE KEY RIGHT AFTER TALKING TO
YOU ON FRIDAY. I THINK I'M BEING FOLLOWED.
A BIG GUY WITH A DARK MUSTACHE AND A TEN-
GALLON HAT. I'M NOT SURE. I ALSO MAILED
A PACKAGE TO MY SISTER ELLEN IN PASADENA.
IF YOU GET THIS, CONTACT HER. SHE'S A GOOD
KID. BE SQUARE WITH HER JOHNNY.

JOCKO

P.S. I HOPE TO HELL YOU NEVER GET A CHANCE
TO READ THIS. A GUY HAS TO PLAY IT BIG ONCE
IN HIS LIFE, AND THIS IS MY CHANCE.

A telephone number was scribbled at the bottom: Atlantic 3-5989.

Poor Jocko Quinn. A little louse with big ideas. I almost felt sorry for him.

I went to the nearest public phone booth and dialed the Atlantic number. There was no answer. I searched through the Pasadena phone book, but could find no listing for an Ellen Quinn. I called the operator, but she wouldn't give me the house number from the phone number; it was against company rules. I tried to think of someone I knew with the phone company, but couldn't.

I walked back to my car, got in and sat through a cigarette. Things were beginning to pile up on me. Two men had been killed—when would it be my turn? I had mailed the $5,000 check to the bank that morning; I now had a bank account of slightly over $5,100. Perhaps this game was worth it. I thought of Jocko Quinn and wondered about his sister. I couldn't imagine a woman with Jocko's features.

I got out of the car and went back to the phone. I dialed the Atlantic number for the second time. It was answered on the ninth ring. The voice, thick with drink, was a woman's. No, she said, Ellen wasn't there; she was never there on week-ends; I might try to reach her at NOrmandy 5-3111. I thanked the drunk.

I dialed the Normandy number. A girl's voice, too husky and too deep, answered.

"Ellen Quinn?"

"Yes?"

"Miss Quinn, this is John J. Phelan. I was a friend of your brother's. I'd like—"

She interrupted: "What do you mean, was?"

She didn't know about Jocko. I looked out of the phone booth at a newspaper stand, at the three-deck headline in the first column. Apparently, she didn't read the papers. I decided to give it to her straight.

There was a short gasp from the other end. I heard her clearing her throat.

"How? When?"

"I'd like to see you, Miss Quinn. I can explain it better in person."

She hesitated, then gave me the street address.

It wasn't far away, and I made it in less than ten minutes. The apartment was in a five-story stucco building on Kingsley, just north of Hollywood boulevard. The girl who answered the bell stood there for a moment, quietly surveying me. I knew this couldn't be Ellen Quinn. This girl was eighteen or nineteen, with a thin face, thin arms, thin legs; everything about her came to a point. An unlit cigarette dangled loosely from one

corner of her bright red lips and she snuggled the ab-
breviated nylon housecoat she wore closer to her; she
had nothing else on, and she let me know it.

"Is Miss Quinn in?"

"Just a moment, man," she said. She waved an arm and
I followed her into the room. A couch and a table lined
one wall; the other was taken up by a single unmade bed;
four or five chairs were scattered about in an uncertain
circle. Several oil paintings hung on the wall above the
bed. They were all of nudes, both men and women—
nothing had been left to the imagination. They seemed
amateurish, even to my untrained eye. An easel and a
half-finished canvas stood in the middle of the room,
sharing the spotlight with a single floor lamp with no
shade on it.

"Ellen's fixing up. She'll be right out."

I sat down on the couch. The half-finished canvas
portrayed the young thing with the housecoat lying on
the couch, her knees up in the air, one leg crossed over
the other. The face looked something like hers, but not
much.

"Pretty good, huh, man?" She looked at me for ap-
proval.

"I don't know much about painting," I said.

"Your kind never does, man," she said. "Too many
muscles, that's your trouble. I don't like muscles."

"I don't like smart young things," I said.

She gave me another glance, laughed, and yelled,
"Ellen!" A voice answered from the other room. "That's
too bad about her brother," the girl said. "He was a fat
slob, if you ask me. I didn't like him, not one bit. Some
people are better off dead."

"I guess you're right."

"I'm always right."

I thought to myself that she could live to be a hundred years old and never be right, not this one.

Ellen Quinn came into the room. She was taller than Jocko and, by religious dieting, she could probably keep her weight around 145. Her dark red hair was brushed back from a part in the middle and she had circles under shifting eyes and a habit of wringing her hands together. The hands and the eyes reminded me of Jocko.

"Mr. Phelan?"

I got to my feet, nodding. I looked at the girl in the housecoat. She grimaced painfully.

"I'll toddle into the other room," she said.

"I'm sorry, Patricia," said Ellen Quinn.

"That's okay, honey," said Patricia. "After all, you don't get a dead brother every day in the week. Might as well make the most of it."

I would have enjoyed slapping the thin little face.

Ellen Quinn cleared her throat uncomfortably and we both were silent. She covered the half-finished painting with a vari-colored linen cloth, then sat down, and I did likewise. She played with her hands.

"I'm sorry I have to be the one," I said.

"That's all right. Somebody had to tell me."

"Didn't the police contact you, Miss Quinn?"

She shook her head negatively.

"Didn't you read it in the papers?"

"I never read the papers," she said. "Nothing in them that I care about. Just murders and wars and nothing else. As for the police—" she shrugged, giving the hands a good work out—"I don't think Jocko advertised the fact that I was his sister. We weren't very close."

"I see."

"How was—when—?"

"He was murdered, Miss Quinn. Shot. It happened Friday evening, last night."

She bowed her head and then raised it again. Her eyes were dry.

"I used to work with your brother, Miss Quinn. I saw him late yesterday afternoon."

"How did you know where to find me?"

"Jocko told me."

"He gave you this number?" She sounded surprised.

"No," I said, "he gave me a number in Pasadena. A woman there gave me this number."

"I've told her not to do that."

Ellen Quinn wasn't much upset about her brother's death. Her hands continued to move and she gave me a half-hearted smile.

"I—I usually spend my week-ends here with Patricia. I'm studying to be a painter, and Patricia models for me. It's cheaper that way." Her eyes swept the paintings on the wall. "More convenient, too," she added.

"Aren't you interested in whether or not the police find your brother's killer?"

"Why should I be?"

I didn't know the answer to that one. I took out a cigarette and lit it, stalling for time. Ellen Quinn wasn't exactly what I had expected—but, then, I didn't know what I had expected.

"When were you home last, Miss Quinn?"

"You mean in Pasadena?"

I nodded.

"Friday morning. Yesterday morning. I'm a typist with a law firm downtown. I left there to go to work. I came here straight from work. I do that every week-end." A toilet flushed from somewhere in the apartment and Miss Quinn looked embarrassed. "You must realize, Mr. Phelan, that my brother and I weren't close. We weren't close at all. He left home when I was only eight. I didn't see him again for almost thirteen years and then when I did—well, he seemed almost like a stranger, a complete stranger."

I pulled the letter from my pocket, handed it to her. She read it, then handed it back to me. Her face didn't change.

"I see," she said. "You want the package."

"I think it would be interesting to see what it contains," I said.

"Was my brother mixed up in something dishonest, Mr. Phelan?"

"Why do you ask?"

"I know what kind of man he was," she said.

"To be absolutely frank with you, Miss Quinn," I said, "I'm not sure, one way or the other. I'd have to see the package, see what it contains."

"Then whatever is in the package might be of value?"

"To both of us," I said.

"But it's addressed to me. Jocko says so, in the letter."

A smile slipped across her face and I felt the squeeze coming.

"You read the letter, Miss Quinn," I said. "You can draw your own conclusions."

"I already have, Mr. Phelan." She rose to her feet. "I think that will be all for now."

I rose beside her.

"Look, baby," I said, "I've gone to a lot of trouble for that package."

"Such as killing my brother?"

"Don't be an idiot. Two men have been killed, Miss Quinn. I think both their deaths were caused by that package."

"I think you'd better leave, Mr. Phelan," said Ellen Quinn.

I looked at her and decided to make the fight on my own ground.

"Suit yourself," I said. "I'm in the phone book. When the boogie-man comes around to knock you off, too, give me a call. I might answer."

She smiled at me in a superior fashion, as if I were some kind of a dolt.

7

THE LITTLE FILIPINO LOOKED AT ME out of sleepy brown eyes and informed me that it was two o'clock in the morning; I looked at him out of equally sleepy eyes and told him to go to hell, but stop on the way and tell Miss Harding that I had to see her. He padded off on his little feet. The trip took him ten minutes and I could see why when I followed him back over the route. We hiked through the long living room, along the swimming pool, through a small grove of orange trees, finally coming out to a small one-room house behind the garage. He gave me a respectful bow and disappeared into the darkness.

I went in. The single room smelled like a woman's room should smell. It contained two easy chairs, a TV set, a massive oak desk with a hand-carved matching chair— and a bed, upon which sat Claire Harding. She was dressed in a pair of red pajamas and her feet were tucked under the blankets.

"You have strange habits, Phelan," she said.

"I went through that once," I said, "with your daughter."

"Dianne? She likes you. I can't understand why."

Her eye had swollen and turned a nifty greenish-yellow. She touched it with tender fingers and gave me a smile.

"First black eye I ever had," she said.

"That's nice."

"Like this?" Her arm took in the whole room.

"Cozy."

"I come out here to be alone. Not many men have been here."

I was one of the select few.

There was a bottle of Old Taylor on the desk. I crossed the room to it, helped myself to four fingers. The whiskey burned my stomach and my head began to ache.

"What did you do with that poor little man?" she asked.

"I beat the hell out of him," I said. "I kicked in his head and smashed his nose and twisted his ears."

"I can imagine."

She gave me another quick smile and then got out of bed. She lost herself in the big, oaken chair. I could see the lines on her face, no longer hidden behind careful makeup. For the first time she looked old enough to be Dianne's mother.

"What do you want, Phelan?"

"I want some answers," I said. "I want them now. You've hired two men before me to find out about your husband. Both of those men are dead. One of them was murdered for sure. I think the other one was, too, though I can't be positive about it."

"You mean Harry Dexter?"

"I mean Harry Dexter."

"But —"

"No buts about it, baby." I was getting mad. "He was strictly the non-drinking type. His wife told me that, just this evening. Dexter was found dead in a car, apparently drunk. I don't think the police are satisfied about it. I know damned well I'm not."

Her hand massaged the back of her neck. She studied me carefully.

"Ask your questions, Phelan."

"Do you know a Harold G. Thompson?"

She started to laugh, and then stopped it. "I should," she said. "He was my second husband. Why?"

"The man out at Malibu was following you. He was hired by Thompson to do so."

"Harold was always jealous. I don't think he's ever gotten over our divorce. He's a writer. He's funny. He still calls occasionally, still tries to ring the bell. He gives me the willies."

"Why would he want to have you followed?"

"That I can't answer. I wouldn't know."

I let that go. Maybe it was just a coincidence. I moved about the room, fighting fatigue. I looked at the bottle of Old Taylor, debating a third drink. I decided against it.

"Tell me about your husband."

"What is there to tell? He's a perfect sonofabitch. I hate his guts."

"Where did you meet him?"

She had to think about that.

"It was a little over four years ago," she said at last. "I was making a picture in England. One of those whodunit things—quite good, too, but it flopped at the box office. My marriage to Walter Thore was on its last legs and—well, Harrison appealed to me. He did have his points."

"When were you married?"

"About six months after we met. I got a Reno divorce from Walter and Harrison and I flew to Mexico City for our marriage. It was all very romantic."

"I can see."

I thought back to Jean MacNeece's description of her —a bitch. Maybe Jean was right. The snake pit.

"What did you know about Woodward? I mean, before you met him."

"Nothing, actually. He was married once before, to an Austrian ballet dancer—or was she German? I can't remember. He'd been divorced for some time. I don't think it's important, but Dianne introduced us."

She threw it out, just like that.

"Dianne? Your daughter?"

"What other Dianne is there? She had just finished school in Switzerland and she brought him along to England with her. I think he taught a course in drama, or some such thing, at her school. I took an immediate liking to him, even got him a small part in my picture. He'd had some previous acting experience." She looked at me and smiled. "He's a lousy actor. You don't think this trouble goes back that far, do you?"

"I don't even know what the hell the trouble is," I said. "And the way things are going I may never find out."

She made the long reach for the Old Taylor and a glass, poured an inch or so, drank it down like an old pro.

"I'll be frank with you, Phelan," she said. "I'll tell you the whole story, just because you're so damned cute and just because it's my money that's paying you. I think Harrison is in some kind of financial trouble."

"What makes you think that?"

She gave me a profile; it was incongruous with the swollen, discolored eye and the swollen lips. I wondered what her millions of fans would think, seeing her like this. She was human, after all.

"I first became suspicious," she said, "a few months ago. I lost a diamond brooch worth about twenty-five thousand dollars. I was going to call the police, but Harrison was adamantly against it. He said the brooch would turn up sooner or later. Then, shortly after that, a valuable ring disappeared. Believe me, I was burned up. Harrison hadn't been working for some time and—" she sighed, giving me a cautious look—"you know how it is in Hollywood. Anyway, I went to him and asked him if he needed any money. At first he denied knowing anything about the missing jewelry, but he finally broke down and confessed that he had sold both pieces. It seems he had lost a great deal of money gambling."

"Had he gambled much before that?"

"Why, no." She looked surprised. "As a matter of fact, he doesn't go in for that sort of thing."

"Didn't you think it funny that he would, quite suddenly, lose a great deal of money gambling?"

"I didn't then. I do now."

"Go on, Miss Harding."

"That's about all there was to it, at that time. But about a month or so later I noticed that some securities we had had in both of our names had been sold. He again told me it was a gambling debt. That time I really flipped my lid. It was in all the columns that we were contemplating a divorce. I'm a fairly wealthy woman, Phelan, but I can't afford a husband who just throws it away."

"How much did he throw away?"

"You mean with the securities and the jewelry?"

I nodded.

"About seventy-five thousand dollars."

That was a long way from $250,000. I wondered if Jocko Quinn had stretched a point—with him, it was possible. With him, anything had been possible.

"So you hired a private detective to trail your husband, to find out where all this money was going?"

"That's right. I hired Harry Dexter. He had done something for a friend of mine and was well recommended. I was surprised when he was killed in that auto accident—" her eyes searched my face—"but I didn't think there was any connection. I still don't. Harrison has his faults, but he's no murderer."

"Did Dexter learn anything?"

"Not much. Only that Harrison was keeping some girl. A young girl." The words were bitter.

"Did he tell you who it was?"

"Yes. She had some ungodly name." She hesitated, apparently searching her mind, but she was fooling only herself. "Bethke. That was it. Helen Bethke."

"Why didn't you tell me all this before, about the gambling and the girl, Helen whatever-her-name-is?"

"Bethke. Helen Bethke. Well, to tell you the truth, Phelan, Jocko Quinn came up with a different story. I hired him about two weeks after Dexter was killed in that accident. He worked on it for a while, then suddenly quit. He told me Harrison wasn't doing anything wrong, that I was wasting my money. I didn't know which of them to believe, so I hired you."

I knew which of them I believed.

"You could have saved us a lot of trouble by telling me this before," I said.

"There's no use in going into that now," she said.

"Did you ever see this Helen Bethke?"

She shook her head.

"Who lives at seven-oh-nine Crescent Way, in Santa Monica?"

Her fingers touched at the swollen eye again.

"You get around, Phelan," she said.

"Helen Bethke lives there," I said, answering my own question. "You went there before meeting Dianne and me at the cabin, and found Woodward, didn't you?"

"I did. I wanted to have it out with him, and with this girl. She wasn't there, though. He was alone. We had words, many of them, and then he beat the hell out of me. Damn him! He'll never do that again."

She rose to her feet, hunched her shoulders up in little-girl fashion, and yawned. She was growing bored. She moved across to the bed, pulled back the blankets and climbed in. I walked over, standing above her, looking down at her. She rolled her eyes at me.

"Come on in," she said, "the sheets are fine."

"You're too old for me," I said.

"Louse," she said, and meant it.

She rolled over on her side, showing me her back.

I slammed the door on my way out.

8

THE NIGHT AIR WAS COOL. I SAT DOWN
in a lawn chair beside the heart-shaped swimming pool.
I thought of many things and also nothing. I had the
$5,000. It would buy me a ticket to any place in the
world I wanted to reach. I owed nothing to Claire
Harding—or did I?

The water lapped sleepily against the side of the
swimming pool and, for one brief moment, I was on an
ocean liner, doing nothing, wanting nothing. Life was
uneventful, simple and straight. The kind of life you
would expect a Woodward to be leading.

"Thinking, Mr. Phelan?"

The words registered somewhere within me. I let them
lie there a moment, then turned in the chair, seeing his
outline against the house behind him. He moved into the
shimmering half-light of the pale moon and the green
water.

Harrison Woodward seemed taller than I remembered
him to be. He looked like the popular conception of a
middle-aged leading man—slacks, sports coat, white silk
scarf, expensive meerschaum pipe, correctly gray at the
temples.

"I distrust young men who sit beside swimming pools

in the early hours of the morning, Mr. Phelan," he said. His tobacco had a sweet, almost pungent, odor to it. "I've been waiting for you."

"You're a patient man," I said.

"One of my few virtues. It has taken me a great deal of time and effort to cultivate it."

I raised a hand in the direction of the cabin, and asked, "How did you know I would come out?"

"You seem to forget, Mr. Phelan, that my wife and I have shared many a bed. I know her habits. To be quite frank, Mr. Phelan—and I'm sure you can verify this—Claire is among the best when it comes to sex. But after it is over, she likes to sleep alone."

A bird chattered its rude awakening from a nearby tree; another one answered.

"You don't mind my having been in there?"

He looked puzzled. "Why should I?"

If he didn't know, I wasn't the one to tell him. A strange set of morals these people had. What had Dianne said?

If it hadn't been so late, if I hadn't been so tired, I would have enjoyed denting his pretty nose.

"And how did you find my dear wife?"

I said: "Bruised. Battered. If I were you, Woodward, I'd stay out of her way for a few days. I think she's the kind that carries a grudge."

"Yes," he said, "she has a simple mind." He laughed; the sound was small and unnatural. "A woman needs an occasional beating, Mr. Phelan. It helps mold her character. You should feel honored at having made the inner sanctum. I haven't been back there in weeks."

"I doubt seriously you'll ever be back there again."

He shrugged. It didn't seem to make much difference to him.

"If I were a simple man of the flesh, Mr. Phelan, Claire would be the end of my search. Unfortunately, I happen to possess a mind, too, a mind which demands a mental existence as well as a physical one."

That was one way of putting it.

I struggled to my feet. They hurt. Everything about me hurt.

"Look, Woodward," I said, "it's been nice. But I've had a long day. I'm tired, bushed, beat, and I don't feel like standing around out here and going through this cheap dialogue."

"Perhaps," he said, "it doesn't have to be cheap. I might make it worth your while."

"You might."

I looked at him. I had been wondering when he would get around to it. I would not have to wait much longer, it seemed.

I followed him back through the house. We ended up in the library. Woodward sat down behind the massive desk, upon which a chessboard was set up. I picked up the White king. It was delicately carved from light wood; it had a fat little Oriental face and a protruding stomach. It was an expensive piece of wood-carving, weighted with lead.

"You play the game, Mr. Phelan?"

"Off and on. Mostly off."

He picked up a pawn in each hand, shuffled his hands back and forth, and stuck them out at me. I tapped the right one; it opened, revealing a White pawn.

"Let's play a game while we chat," he said.

I had nothing to lose: nothing, that is, except my sleep, my health, and, quite possibly, my life.

I moved a chair up beside the desk. I made my usual opening move with the king's pawn.

He smiled, and said, "No imagination, Mr. Phelan. No imagination."

But he duplicated my opening move.

I developed my king's knight.

He kept his eyes on the chessboard. One hand fluttered over it, then went back to his side. "I don't like being followed, Mr. Phelan," he said.

I thought of Mannie Mendosa. A queer little sensation hit my stomach. Mannie had a sweet wife and two little kids. If anything had happened to him . . .

He moved his queen's knight.

"Don't worry about your Mr. Mendosa," he said, reading my thoughts. "He's quite safe. He and I had a small talk about the error of his following me. I imagine he is at home now, sleeping safely with his wife. If he has a wife."

"Did you talk to him like you did to Dexter and Quinn?"

His eyes lifted to a level with mine.

"That's unkind, Mr. Phelan. Very unkind."

"I'm known as an unkind bastard in the trade, Woodward. But both of them preceded me in this job. Both of them are dead."

"Quite so."

It didn't seem to disturb him.

He said, "Please believe me when I say that I had nothing to do with their deaths. Absolutely nothing, on my word."

"I have a strange habit of believing only one man in this world, Woodward. His name happens to be John J. Phelan. I've found he's the only one I can trust."

"Ah," he said, the noise coming from deep within his throat. "And a cynic, too. You know, Mr. Phelan, under other circumstances and in other times, I feel that we might have grown fond of one another."

"I doubt it."

"But—" he started.

"Can it," I said. "Get to the point."

I developed my king's bishop, threatening his queen's knight.

"A fair move," he said. "It shows your complete disregard for the bishop. You are willing to sacrifice him in order to take my knight which, on the surface, appears to be an even trade. But, is it? I wonder if you would be so willing to sacrifice a human life?"

I merely looked at him. He had a habit of avoiding a direct look. It was a habit that annoyed me.

He held a match over the pipe; the sweet odor wafted over to me.

"I like a man who plays a forceful game," he said, "whether it's in chess or in life. I remember a tournament in Geneva some years back in which I played the great Borovsky—perhaps you are familiar with him? I made exactly the same three opening moves you have just made. Unfortunately, I lost the game." His hand hovered over the chessboard. "How much is Claire paying you to find out about me?"

"Enough," I said.

He moved his king's knight.

"A very evasive answer, Mr. Phelan. Not at all like

you. You are a direct man. Enough is a relative amount, depending upon the person."

"You figure it out," I said.

I moved my queen's pawn.

"And now you go back to caution," he said. "That disappoints me. Regardless of the amount, I will match it. Life will be easier for you."

"You mean just to quit working for your wife?"

"I mean to get the money back for me."

I studied him. His face was handsome and calm. The chin line was well formed and there was no hint of weakness there. He was a careful man, hiding behind his mask of useless words. I imagined him to be completely unbothered by the usual human sentiments. He would hold his life to a definite pattern—anything that interfered with that pattern would be relentlessly removed.

"What money?"

His laughter seemed genuine.

"The two hundred and fifty thousand," he said.

He moved his queen's knight back in front of his king; it was an unorthodox move. It surprised me.

"I don't know what you're talking about, Woodward," I said.

"Oh, come now," he said, "don't underestimate me. At least grant me the courtesy of not doing that. Let's keep the game to the one on the chessboard. The late Jocko Quinn had a quarter of a million in his possession some time before he was killed. I would like that money."

"Who wouldn't?"

"You are misunderstanding the whole thing, Mr. Phelan."

Perhaps I was. At that time of morning, I could have misunderstood anything.

"If Quinn had that kind of money," I said, "and it belonged to you, we'd have motive enough for murder."

"Of course we would," he said. "I agree to that. But, as I said, I had nothing to do with Quinn's death. Absolutely nothing." The quick smile hid something deep within him. "I won't deny that I would have enjoyed wringing his fat little neck. The idea appealed to me. He caused me no little trouble. I've been honest with you so far. I'll continue to be. You see, Mr. Phelan, I had possession of the money at one time, but it does not belong to me. The money was merely in my safe-keeping. My life has been endangered since I lost it."

I wondered who would be dumb enough to entrust $250,000 to Harrison Woodward. He had the kind of charm and personality and looks that might flutter the heart of some middle-aged female, but I had the idea this wasn't the case.

I took his king's pawn with my king's knight.

He smiled lightly, moving his queen's bishop pawn.

"In other words," I said, "you want me to quit working for your wife and go to work for you."

"I need help. I don't deny it. Also, there are certain things in my private life I don't want Claire to know about."

"Like Helen Bethke?"

His eyes moved slowly across my face.

"I didn't know you knew about Helen."

"I get around."

"I guess you do."

I moved my king's knight.

"You're not paying attention to the game, Mr. Phelan. That was quite a stupid move." He took my king's bishop with his pawn. "Perhaps I am overestimating you."

"It doesn't matter," I said.

I moved my king's knight a second time. It was a simple plan. It had worked often for me in the past. It was available in any dollar edition on chess.

"Check and checkmate," I said.

He looked astounded. He studied the board a full thirty seconds, then suddenly slammed his closed fist down on the desk, knocking some of the men over. He rose to his feet, pacing about the room.

Playing the part of a good loser was not one of his virtues.

I watched him, and then said, "It's no dice, Woodward. I have a peculiar habit of working for one client at a time. Your wife hired me first. I'll stick to that."

"You're allowing sentiment to interfere with your business sense."

I shrugged.

"I said I'd make it worth your while."

"I imagine you would," I said. "But I'm not interested."

"You're making a mistake."

"Like I did in the chess game?"

The look he gave me was hard. It was the first time he had looked directly into my eyes.

I stood up.

"Mr. Phelan," he said, "I went to the trouble of checking on Jocko Quinn. He was a completely unlikable person, one who had been mixed up in various dirty dealings. He had not a friend in the world. You, as his ex-working partner, are the only one he could have turned to in time of stress. I think you know where that money is. I intend to get it back."

I said, "If it weren't so late, I'd knock your teeth down your throat."

He shrugged and his fingers played with the white silk scarf. "All right," he said, "have it your way. I tried peaceful means. Remember that. My back is against the wall, Mr. Phelan. Good night."

My head was spinning and my body ached. It was a long drive home.

PART II

The Exposed

9

THE SPARROW AND THE FLY LOOKED AT
each other from opposite sides of the window screen; the
sparrow cocked his head to one side, gave the screen a
tentative peck with his bill, then gave up and flew away.

I rolled over in bed, kicking the blankets away. The
day was already getting warm. My clock said 10:20.
A Sunday morning like all other Sunday mornings when
you wake up alone. The fog drifted through my head
and I felt heavy throughout.

The telephone continued to ring in the other room. I
finally got up and answered it.

Mannie Mendosa said, "*Amigo.*"

I said, "You should go back to fighting four-rounders."

"I'm sorry."

"You should be."

"How did you know about it?"

"I talked to Woodward last night."

"Gabby guy, ain't he?"

I said he was.

"He's a smart one, *amigo.* Very smart."

I said, "Did you find out anything at all about him?"

"Not much. I followed him from the house in Beverly
Hills to a bar on Ventura out in the valley. A real plush

place. Nothin' but big Caddies in the parking lot. It's called The Golden Arrow. Some guy came out of the bar and told me Woodward wanted to see me. I guess I screwed the works."

"Don't worry about it, Mannie. I've got another job for you."

I gave him Ellen Quinn's description and the address on Kingsley. He promised to do better this time. I hoped he would. I was positive she would lead me to the money.

After talking to Mannie, I let a cold shower clear away the rest of the fog. I read the follow-up news story on Jocko Quinn's murder in *The Times* over four scrambled eggs and six pieces of bacon. The story was buried on page six of the second news section. The police department attributed the killing to something in Quinn's past.

After breakfast I dialed Jean MacNeece at home. I said, "It's time for all little girls to be up and about."

"I'm not a good little girl, you louse. I need my beauty sleep."

"On you, angel, it's wasted."

"What?"

"You're already beautiful."

"Okay," she said. "Who do you want to know about this time?"

"Two people," I said. "The first is Harold G. Thompson."

She laughed, then said, "Claire Harding's second husband. A writer. Used to be pretty good, I think. Now he writes for the cleft-conscious crowd. He and Harding have been divorced almost ten years now, and rumor has it he still hasn't gotten over her. Rumor also has it he's gotten a bit on the queer side. For what it's worth, I don't believe the second rumor."

"You are an angel, angel."

"I'm sprouting wings, right now. Come on over and see. I'm not wearing much else."

I said, "The thought frightens me."

"Thanks. What's the other biography?"

"Helen Bethke."

She let out her breath, and said, "The way you say the name, she must be some dish."

"I've never seen her."

"I've never heard of her. I'll keep my ear to the ground, though."

"Thanks."

I hung up.

I put on a clean shirt and a light brown gabardine suit and went down to the rented Plymouth. I drove down Melrose towards Wilshire, cutting down a side street near Highland. A plaincothes cop with his face stuck in a newspaper was parked in a Ford in front of Jocko Quinn's apartment, so I kept going. I wanted, eventually, to get a look at Jocko's apartment. I didn't know what I expected to find.

I got on Wilshire and started towards Santa Monica, letting my mind idle over the past forty-eight hours. I had met a legend in the flesh, Claire Harding. Harrison Woodward? I wondered if his attempt to buy me off the previous night was actually on the level; it probably was. Dianne? Dianne Cochran. Dianne of the long legs and the wide, tempting mouth and the short black hair—I had to stop that. Ellen Quinn? I felt a little nauseated. But she would lead me to the $250,000, of that I was sure. I hoped that Mannie Mendosa was keeping awake.

On its surface, the case was quite simple—$250,000 had been stolen from Harrison Woodward. That the money was not his would explain his hocking Claire's jewelry and securities. But he had been hocking things long before Jocko Quinn showed up on the scene, or even Harry Dexter.

One question needed an answer—whose money was the quarter million? When I found the answer to that I felt reasonably certain I would find the person who had killed both Dexter and Quinn.

There were only four million people in and around Los Angeles. Not bad odds.

Crescent Way ran parallel with Wilshire in Santa Monica. I found 709 easily enough, just eight blocks east of the ocean. The house was in a quiet, old neighborhood of two- and three-story apartments, with ROOMS FOR RENT signs on every one of them. 709, however, didn't fit in with the rest. It was long and low and quite modernistic and stuck out like a sixth finger.

I parked and watched a kid with a pimply face and a ducktail haircut work half-heartedly with a lawnmower.

Finally I got out of the car and walked over to him.

I said, "Lousy day to be working."

"You tellin' me?" he said. He leaned against the handle of the mower. "You got a butt on you, mister?"

I gave him a cigarette, then held the match for him. He inhaled, coughed lightly, and looked embarrassed. He turned around to look at the house behind him, apparently satisfying himself that no one was watching him. He was tall and thin and nervous. His hands kept moving about, and I tried to avoid looking at the mass of pimples.

"You know the people in seven-oh-nine?" I asked.

"Some," he said.

"I'm looking for a young woman," I said. "Helen Bethke."

The nervousness increased in his eyes. The hands continued to move, and he took another drag on the cigarette, then licked his lips.

"Yeh," he said, "I wouldn't mind lookin' for her myself. You a cop?"

"No," I said.

He looked back at the house again.

"She's sure some dish, mister," he said.

"She home now?"

"I ain't seen her today."

I imagined that he kept quite an eye out for her, too.

"Thanks, buddy," I said. "Don't work too hard."

"Don't worry about me."

I wouldn't.

I left the kid with his cigarette and his pimples and his dreams and went over to 709. The foyer was done nicely in black chipped marble; one wall contained six mail boxes. Helen Bethke was in Apartment B. I rang the buzzer. Nothing happened. I read the other names on the mail boxes. They didn't mean anything to me. Apartment A's card read, MAUD DOHENY, MANAGER. I rang that buzzer and the door clicked open immediately. I entered the hallway.

The door to Apartment A opened and was blocked by a young girl in a wheelchair. We studied each other. She had corn-yellow hair, folding back from a wide forehead in loose waves, intelligent blue eyes, and a

cheerful, sunny smile. She could have been anything between sixteen and twenty-two. I looked down at the
red Indian blanket covering her legs. She followed my
glance.

"Hello," I said. "I don't mean to be rude."

"You mean about looking at my legs?"

I nodded. I felt embarrassed.

"You're not rude," she said. Her voice was low and
husky and had charm. She added: "Hi," and we both
laughed.

"Is your mother in?" I asked.

"I don't have one," she said. "Not now. I live here
with my aunt. Aunt Maud. She manages these apartments. She isn't in, though. But perhaps I could help
you."

"Perhaps you could," I said. "I'm looking for Helen
Bethke. She doesn't seem to answer her buzzer."

"She wouldn't," the girl said. "She isn't in."

"I'm having all kinds of luck," I said. "You wouldn't
happen to know where I could locate Miss Bethke, would
you? It's important."

"No," she said. "She went away for the week-end. I
don't know where." Her fingers played with the spokes
of the wheel chair. "Besides, it isn't Miss Bethke, it's
Mrs."

"Oh," I said.

"Are you a policeman?"

"Sort of," I said. "A private detective."

She looked interested.

"Why don't you come in?" She gave me one of those
cheerful, sunny smiles. "I'm all alone. I'll be glad to
answer your questions. I'm sure you have a lot of them

to ask. Besides, I have nothing else to do. It's too early for television."

I had nothing to lose.

She swung the chair around expertly, and I followed her into the apartment. It was furnished in good taste, if you like modern, which I don't. Everything was neat and in its proper place; I felt like an intruder. Everything was feminine, too.

Something squawked loudly behind me, and I jumped, startled. The girl laughed as I turned around.

"Herman doesn't like you, either," she said.

A parrot, its red, green, and yellow feathers dulled by age, gave me a cold stare from the safety of a brass bird cage. I gave him a cold stare in return. I thought he won.

"Aunt Maud's parrot," she said. "He hates me. I think Herman is getting pretty old. I think he's outlived his usefulness. Someday, I'm going to wring his neck and feed him to the cat. Herman, I mean."

I got what she meant.

"My name is Phelan," I said.

"Agnes Doheny," she said. "I'm pleased to meet you, Mr. Phelan." Her head bowed and lifted again. The hair was soft and silky, real nice. "Please, sit down. I don't get to talk to people often, being a cripple. I enjoy talking, too."

I sat down. "I'll bet you do," I said.

"But it isn't so bad," she said.

I made a temple with my hands in front of my face; I don't know why.

"What made you think I was a policeman?" I asked.

"Well," she said, "the other two men that were here asking about Mrs. Bethke are both dead now. I figured that something was funny about that. I figured the police would be around."

"You're a smart kid," I said.

"Thank you," she said. "But I'm not a kid."

She wasn't, I realized.

"You can smoke if you like," she said. "It doesn't bother me."

I took out my pipe. I tamped in tobacco, then lit it. She laughed.

"What's so funny?"

"That," she said. She laughed again. "I saw you talking to Bobbie Hooper outside, through the window. I made a bet with myself that you would come in here asking about Mrs. Bethke. I also made a bet that you would smoke a pipe."

"You could have cheated," I said. "I was smoking in the car."

"I could have," she said, "but I didn't."

She *was* a smart one. I liked her.

I could hear the clacking of the lawn mower outside. Apparently, the kid with the pimples had decided to do some work.

"Well," she said, "you can ask your questions."

Just like that.

I started. "Tell me about the two men that were here. The two that are dead now."

"The first one was Mr. Dexter. He was quite nice. I liked him. I answered his questions for him. He wanted to know all about Mrs. Bethke, her visitors, you know, like that. I was sorry when I read about his accident in the papers."

I don't know why I said it, but I did. "It wasn't an accident. At least, I don't think it was."

Her blue eyes widened into a pair of saucers. She scratched the back of one hand with the fingers of the other.

"You mean—"

"Uh-huh," I said.

She shuddered, and crossed her hands in front of her.

"Tell me about the other one," I said.

She looked at me. She thought a minute, then said: "Well, I didn't know his name at first, not until I saw his picture in yesterday's paper. Jocko Quinn. He had body odor and smoked a horrible smelling cigar. I didn't like the way he looked at me. I felt like he was undressing me with his eyes. Even me."

Even her.

"Yes," I said.

"But that was horrible, the way he was killed. How could anyone do such a thing? I don't know what gets in people's minds."

"Neither do I, honey," I said.

I thought of all the horrible things in the world—God knows, there were enough of them to think about. Here was one sweet little flower, unblemished, untouched, adding a breath of freshness.

We let the silence go along for a while. I got up, finally, and walked to the window. The kid with the pimples was resting again. He had been joined by another kid, and they were sitting on the lawn, looking through a magazine. I had an idea what kind of magazine it was. Good kids, those.

I turned around. "Does Mr. Bethke live here?"

"Oh, no," Agnes said. "He was killed in Korea."

I thought it would be something like that.

"Do they call you a shamus, or a private eye, or a private dick?" she asked.

"Those," I said, "and other things, too."

"Gee," she said. Her fingers played a silent tune on the spokes of the wheelchair. "You know, Mr. Phelan, I bet I know what all the trouble is."

With her, I wouldn't bet.

"What, Agnes?"

"Well," she said, "understand me now. I like Mrs. Bethke. Very much. She's been quite nice to me, and to my aunt. But I think she plays around a lot. With men, I mean."

I knew what she meant.

She said, "I'll bet you been hired by someone's wife."

I said, "If you ever need a job, look me up."

Her laughter was warm and the kind that spread around you, yet touched you inside.

"Tell me about Helen Bethke."

"Well," she said, "she's in her mid-twenties. Very attractive and well built. I'd guess her at about a thirty-eight, twenty-four, thirty-four." She smiled embarrassedly at me, then looked away. "She has blonde hair, wears it long down to her shoulders, and is a very neat dresser. She has a warm, nice personality."

"What does she do for a living?"

"That," she said, "I don't know. With her looks and figure, though, she could be connected with the movies or television. I've never heard her mention a job, though. Gee, Mr. Phelan, I like her. I hope she isn't mixed up in anything too bad."

"I don't know," I said. "Not yet."

"That's not quite true," she said.

"What isn't?"

"About her job."

"Well?"

"I—" she hesitated, fumbling with her words—" I think she might be a prostitute."

I tried not to laugh. The way she said it was that funny. "A what?" I said.

She blushed. "A prostitute. You know, Mr. Phelan."

Yes I knew.

She looked at everything in the room, but me.

"I don't blame her, understand," she said. "I'm not even sure about it. It's just an idea."

"What makes you think it, Agnes?"

"Well," she said, "I've never seen another woman visit her. I know, that's a pretty small thing. But she has men visitors quite a bit. They come around a lot."

"Men like Harrison Woodward?"

"How did you know about him?"

"I get around."

I refilled my pipe and lit it.

"How often does Mr. Woodward come around?"

"Quite a lot. More than the rest."

"He was here yesterday, wasn't he?"

"Yes. But Mrs. Bethke wasn't. And then right after he got here, Claire Harding—you know, the movie star— came, too. They had a terrible fight. It was awful."

A lot of things were awful.

"Tell me about the other men who visit her."

"I don't know any of their names. The other ones, I mean. Just Mr. Woodward." She hesitated, thinking. "I said a lot of men. That's not quite true, either. There are only four that I know about. There's Mr. Woodward. Then there's one that's pretty old—I'd say about sixty or so—and a younger man. I think the younger one might

be Mexican. And the fourth one is the strangest of all.
He wears a big hat, you know, like a cowboy. I've seen
him in the hall, but he never speaks to me. He gives me
the willies."

I thought back to the note from Jocko Quinn. He had
said it was a big guy with a dark mustache and a ten-
gallon hat that had been following him. Maybe Helen
Bethke was more important than I had imagined.

"Agnes," I said, "would you do me one big favor?"

She smiled. "That depends."

"I'd like to get into Mrs. Bethke's apartment."

"I don't know." She turned the wheelchair around.
She looked at Herman, and then at me. "I don't think
Aunt Maud would like that. It's not right."

"No," I said, "it's not right. But it is important."

She looked at me again, but didn't say anything. She
wheeled over to a desk in the corner, rummaged through
it for a moment, then held out a keyring to me.

"Go ahead," she said. "I like you."

"Believe me, honey, it's mutual."

I took the keyring and went into the hallway. There
was no one about. I walked down to Apartment B,
opened the door and went in. The venetian blinds were
pulled shut and the windows had been closed for some
time. The apartment was dark and stuffy. I switched on
a wall light and looked around. It was an exact duplicate of Apartment A, without Herman. That was a
pleasant difference.

A three-tier bookcase in one corner was jammed with
books. There were more books than shelves—someone
had piled about twenty of them against the wall. I read
over some of the titles. The authors included Dos Passos,

Hemingway, Faulkner, Sartre—Helen Bethke had good reading habits.

I went through the drawers of a desk, and found nothing much—an unpaid bill from the telephone company; a piece of scratch paper with the letter H and two arrows below that, written in heavy pencil.

I went into the bedroom. The bed was made, neatly. The blinds were open, letting the sunshine filter in. There was an ashtray on the floor beside the bed. I stooped down, looking at it. It held three cigarette butts and two unsmoked Lucky Strikes.

The top drawer of a bureau contained three pairs of silk hose, a flimsy nightgown, a girdle, and a pair of silk panties with matching brassiere. The color of the panties and the bra was pink. The second drawer contained four green bath towels; the bottom drawer held a pair of men's striped pajamas.

The closet contained two light cotton dresses, a very smart and very expensive grey suit, and a rayon raincoat. No shoes. No hats.

Except for a bar of soap, a face towel, a toothbrush and a tube of toothpaste, the bathroom was empty.

The kitchen contained a coffee pot, but no coffee; four highball glasses, and a bottle of good scotch.

It all added up to something—but what?

I returned to the living room and sat down to think it over. Helen Bethke had strange habits. There was nothing in the room that would definitely identify her, other than the unpaid telephone bill. The apartment hardly looked lived in. That meant it was a front, but a front for what? The rent was high here.

I left the apartment locked and returned to Agnes.

She was sitting in front of the window, soaking up a little sunshine. She gave me that smile.

"Find anything interesting?" she asked.

"Not a thing," I said.

Herman squawked at us again. I could do without him.

I said, "Tell me, Agnes, just how often does Mrs. Bethke stay here?"

"Not too much," she said. "Not more than two or three nights a week."

"Does she ever get any mail?"

"I wouldn't know that."

"Would you do me one more great big favor?"

She smiled her answer.

"When Mrs. Bethke returns, give me a call." I handed her one of my cards. "I'd appreciate it."

"For you, Mr. Phelan," she said, "anything." She blushed again, biting at her lower lip—on her, it was becoming. "Well, almost anything."

I bent down, kissed her lightly on the cheek.

The kid with the pimples was nowhere in sight. A middle-aged man in an undershirt was lazily pushing the lawn mower. He gave me a dirty look. I didn't blame him.

10

THE PARKING ATTENDANT WAS YOUNG; he had a thin, hard mouth, and wore a pale olive uniform with the words, GOLDEN ARROW, printed in gold letters on his back. He saw the U-Drive sticker on the windshield of the Plymouth, gave me a contemptuous glance, and gunned the car around a corner of the lot.

I went into the low, red-brick building with the crushed rock roof. The air-conditioning hit me like a gentle perfume. The blonde hostess was tall and trimly built; she wore a dress that didn't hide much of her, two tiny golden arrows for earrings, and a fixed smile. She offered me a menu, printed in gold lettering, and I shook my head, motioning at the bar.

Everything was gold. It could get a little monotonous.

The bar extended along the right wall in a straight line and was jammed to near-capacity, while the dining room, on the left, was nearly empty. I could hear the soft tinkling of a piano.

The bartender was a fat little guy with a fringe of gray hair around his ears and a perpetual scowl. He tried on a smile for my benefit.

I ordered beer. He poured the glass half-full, so the head was just right, wiped the glass with a wet towel, and set the glass before me with a flourish.

97

He asked, "How is it outside?"

I said. "Sunny. Sunny, and getting hot."

He said, "It's always hot."

He moved away, and I tasted the beer. It was cold and felt good going down. There's nothing like that first beer on a hot day, absolutely nothing.

I got up and took my beer with me to the piano-bar in the back. The girl at the piano had bright red hair, freckled shoulders and a freckled face to go with the hair, and avoiding gray eyes. She caressed the piano keys in a nonchalant manner and drifted along on her own channel. I could see a door marked PRIVATE behind the potted palms.

"Hi," I said.

Her eyes drifted across my face, but didn't stop.

I tried it again.

"Beat it, buster," she said.

"I'm not much good at that," I said.

Her smile was crooked. It gave her face a lopsided appearance.

"Smart, huh?"

"Just enough to get by," I said.

She shifted to another tune without breaking stride.

"You're cute, buster," she said.

"So are you, Red."

Her laughter belonged to another time and another place.

"And original, too. My, my."

"I'm lonely."

"Who ain't, buster?"

I couldn't answer that, not really.

I took out a fresh pack of cigarettes. I stuck one in my mouth and gestured at her with the pack. She opened her mouth and I stashed one in the gaping hole, catching a glimpse of more gold. I lit for both of us; she blew smoke at me.

"Now that we've figured out that you're smart and cute and original," she said, "where do we go?"

"Where would you like to go?"

The freckled shoulders hunched themselves up. "A million miles away."

"I'm your boy."

Her face dimmed behind the clouds of smoke. Gray ash formed on the end of her cigarette. She leaned over the piano, letting the ash fall on it.

"What's exciting?" I asked.

"Depends on what you want."

"Any games around here?"

Interest showed in her eyes. "Feeling reckless?"

"I heard around town you could get an occasional game here," I said. "I got ten new bills in my wallet. I'd like to double 'em."

"And me?"

"After I double the bills."

"What makes you think I'd know about a game?"

She stopped playing, quite suddenly, and stood up. She walked on stiff legs around the potted palms, disappearing through the door marked PRIVATE. I ordered a second beer and was nursing it along when she returned. She sat down at the piano again, taking up where she had left off.

The guy who had followed her out of the door stood next to me. He was in a black pin-stripe suit, black shirt, with a white bowtie; he had the bent, pushed-in nose and funny eyes of a prizefighter. He kept looking at me.

"Any luck?" I asked her.

"Ask Joey."

"Okay, Joey," I said.

"Smart guy?" Joey said.

"I went through that bit with Red," I said.

She laughed, and Joey gave her a dirty look. His hands were big and flat-knuckled. He drummed them along the top of the piano, then made up his mind.

"Come on," he said.

I put a five-dollar bill on the piano. "Thanks, Red," I said.

"Keep me in mind," she said. "But only if you win. I'm expensive."

Joey stood waiting for me with his hands resting on his thighs. I kept looking at those hands. I imagined that he got his kicks out of using them and hoped he wouldn't get the chance on me. I followed him around the potted palms, and he did a slow drum-beat on the door with his flat knuckles. We waited a full minute, then a buzzer sounded and we went in.

The room was wide and deep and plush; everything was done in gray, from the ankle-deep carpet to the face of the man sitting behind the desk at the far end of the room. I recognized the face. I had a small ache in the middle of my back.

There was a gray leather sofa and easy chair. I took a chance on the chair, and watched the man behind the desk. He had small blue eyes that seemed intelligent, the gray face, two chins, and a head of bushy gray hair. He was eating a three-inch thick steak and a hunk of cheese.

"Okay, Joey," he said, and Joey padded out of the room.

"You know me?" The man at the desk asked.

"Sure," I said. "Lou Chiozza. San Quentin, class of forty-seven. Considered bright, fairly legitimate, and you don't go in for rough stuff."

His fat cheeks worked themselves up and down on a piece of steak; he looked at the cheese disinterestedly, but finally put a small hunk in his mouth. He pointed a fork at me.

"And you?" he said.

"Phelan. John J. Phelan."

"Oh," he said. "The shamus."

"Uh-huh."

"I've heard of you, too."

"I've got a reputation."

"What's the idea of coming in here asking for a game? You trying to be bright?"

"No one's ever accused me of being that," I said.

"What do you want?"

"Just nosing around."

"Well, nose some place else."

"Anything you say, Lou."

I got to my feet. I studied the charcoal caricatures of sports notables on the walls. They weren't bad. They included a couple of people I knew.

"Wait a minute," he said.

He pushed the plate away from him. He dabbed at his mouth with a white linen napkin, then stood. He came around the corner of the desk. He was no taller than five-five. He took out a long, thin cigar and stuck it in his mouth, but didn't light it.

"Shamus," he said, "I think we're on opposite teams."

"That could be."

"You had Harrison Woodward tailed out here last night. Why?"

"That's a good question."

"I'd like a good answer."

I said nothing to that, and he finally sat on the corner of the desk, lighting his cigar. He swung one leg back and forth, staring at the toe of his shoe.

"Woodward's wife after him?"

"You might say that. And then again you might not."

"Don't give me a hard time, Phelan. I don't like it."

"You can go to hell, Lou."

His hand ran across the top of the desk; one finger raised itself above the others, came down on a buzzer. We didn't have to wait long for Joey to join us. He looked at me out of those funny eyes. I looked at his flat-knuckled hands.

"Look, Phelan," said Chiozza, "let's be reasonable. We're both considered intelligent. Let's act like it. Woodward came out here last night. We're old friends. You had a tail on him, and I want to know why."

"It's personal."

"You're a stubborn bastard, aren't you?"

"Depends on how you look at it."

The silence became thick. I ankled through the deep carpet over to the door. Joey stood there like an obedient dog; I put out a hand and he slapped it aside. The slap stung. I turned back to Chiozza.

"Was it your money, Lou?"

The blue eyes snapped at me. Lou moved away from the desk.

"What are you talking about, shamus?"

"I think you know."

We let that ride for a moment. I could hear Joey breathing behind me; his breath came in short jolts.

"Don't get in too deep," Chiozza said.

"I'm already in," I said. "It's either sink or swim now. Two guys are dead in this job, Lou. I don't think you go in for that sort of thing. However, the ante is pretty high. You might have changed your habits—I wouldn't know."

"What two guys?"

I laughed in his face.

"Joey," Chiozza said, "remind me about this guy some time. Remind me that I don't like him."

Joey only grunted. In his job, he didn't have to talk.

I moved back to the door. Chiozza nodded and Joey stepped aside, allowing me to pass. I squeezed by him and through the doorway. I made it around the potted palms. That feeling in the middle of my back had moved forward—now, both my back and stomach ached. But I had found out what I had wanted to know—Lou Chiozza was in it with Woodward, whatever it was.

I exchanged winks with Red on the way out. She looked disappointed in me.

11

IT WAS ALMOST SIX O'CLOCK WHEN I got back to my apartment and called my answering service. There were no messages. I felt slightly disappointed. I wanted to meet Helen Bethke.

I took off my coat, loosened my tie and went into the bedroom. When I switched on the light, something about the room bothered me. I stood there a few minutes, looking around me. I finally saw what it was—various small objects had been disturbed, as if someone not familiar with the place had spent some time there.

One of the pillows was lying in the middle of the bed, a dark smudge about the size of a grapefruit on one corner. I walked across and picked up the pillow. The smudge was blood. I put the pillow down and went into the bathroom.

Ellen Quinn was in the bathtub. A fly trotted across her forehead, but she didn't seem to mind. My hands got sweaty, and something like terror took hold of my vitals.

I stood beside the bathtub and looked down at her— her head was arched crazily to one side, her lips were swollen and bruised. She had not only been murdered— someone had methodically worked her over. There was no use in my going into details—those were for the cops.

I remember thinking that someone a lot rougher than I was looking for that loose quarter-million.

I left Ellen Quinn like that and went back through the apartment into the kitchen. I got out a bottle of Four Roses and took a long slug, then another. My hands were jumpy. I took another slug to calm them, then set the bottle down, and went downstairs. I talked to Mrs. Whiting, the house manager. I asked her if she had seen anyone come up to my apartment while I was out—she hadn't. She remarked that I didn't look so well and I agreed with her. She looked at me, scenting trouble, so I went back upstairs.

In the bedroom, I removed the pillows from both cases, ripped the sheets off the bed. I tore the laundry marks out of one sheet, then took the other sheet and the two pillowcases and went down the backstairs to the incinerator. I stood there while the two pillowcases and the sheet burned into nothingness; I had to be sure.

I walked around to the front of the apartment and, standing in shadow, surveyed the street. Two cars went by. One of them made a slow U-turn at the corner and came by again. I stood there until its taillights had disappeared. I crossed the street, got the rented Plymouth, and drove it around through the alleyway to the side entrance of the apartment. I turned off the motor, unlocked the trunk of the car, and went back upstairs.

I put the sheet with the missing laundry marks on the floor, and then got Ellen Quinn out of the bathtub. It was quite a job. I put her down on the sheet, then rolled the sheet around her.

I picked her up, tilting the dead weight over one shoulder. I got as far as my front door when I heard someone in the hallway outside. There were giggling

noises and another sound which I couldn't recognize—
I waited. The dead weight was getting heavy on my
shoulder. I opened the door an inch, then two inches.
No one was outside. I carried the body downstairs and
put it in the trunk of the car. I closed the trunk, but
didn't lock it. I got in the front seat. My hands were
jumpy again—it took me three tries to get the key into
the ignition.

I drove out towards Griffith Park.

I dumped the body on a side road leading to the
observatory. No one saw me. I was sure. At least, I
thought I was sure. I kept the car on the paved road,
and made sure I didn't get my feet off on to the soft
shoulders. They could trace tire tracks; they could trace
footprints.

I drove back to Hollywood and the Kingsley address.
Mannie Mendosa's car squatted right across from the
dead Miss Quinn's apartment.

He got out of the car, leaning against the hood, staring at me.

"*Amigo*," he said, "you don't look so good."

"I don't feel so good, Mannie," I said.

"What's up?"

"Nothing," I said. "Anything happen here?"

"Nothing, *amigo*, nothing. I've been here since you
called this morning. Ellen Quinn hasn't left the apartment. I've been watching real good."

Yeah, real good.

"Okay, Mannie," I said, "forget about it. Also, forget
about the whole job. No one has to know you were out
here."

"You're the boss," he said. He looked at me again.
"You don't look so good, *amigo*."

"You said that before."

"Yeh."

"Run along, Mannie."

He got into his car. I watched him drive away, then walked across the street to the apartment building.

Patricia had on the same housecoat she had worn the last time I saw her; the only difference in her appearance was a little rouge and a new coat of lipstick.

She stood in the doorway, clutching at the housecoat. She looked worried. "Man," she said, "you look beat."

"I want to talk," I said.

"Ellen isn't here."

"Oh?"

She gave me a tentative smile, then erased it.

"You better run along, man," she said.

I pushed her aside and walked into the apartment. Nothing had changed. Everything was the same. The same lousy paintings, the same lousy furniture. Only Ellen Quinn would never see it again.

"Where'd she go?" I wanted to hear her story.

"Man," she said, "you annoy me."

I slapped her hard, once across the face. The force of the slap knocked her back into the easel, knocking it over. She looked down at the easel, then up at me. She nibbled at the fresh coat of lipstick, ruining it.

"You muscle-guys are all alike," she said. "I don't like muscles."

"Where'd she go?"

"I don't know." She nibbled at the lipstick some more. "Man," she said, "to be honest with you, I'm worried."

"Why?"

"A woman came by, right after you left last night. I was in the back room. I heard her and Ellen talking.

When I came out, Ellen had her hat and coat on, and said she had to run along for a minute. She didn't look right, though. She hasn't been back since."

It sounded true. It probably was. I had no reason to doubt it.

"Okay," I said, "who was this woman? What did she look like?"

"I never saw her before. She was tall, blonde, good-looking, if you like that type."

Helen Bethke. Maybe.

"Okay, baby," I said, "thanks."

"Hey," she said, "what the hell's this all about?"

"I don't know."

"The hell you don't."

We gave each other a couple of hard stares.

She said, "I knew that fat bastard of a brother of her's would cause us a lot of trouble."

She didn't know how much trouble.

I went back to my own apartment again. I didn't know what I intended to do. Nothing, I guess. Someone was sure making a first-class pigeon out of me. They had dumped Jocko Quinn's body in my car, and now they had dumped his sister's body in my bathtub.

I opened the door, and went in.

Rossi had been watching for me. He smiled and took two short steps toward me. I saw the punch coming, but was too late ducking. His fist caught me on the side of the head, and I spun around, crashing into the wall. He slugged me twice in the kidneys, then stepped back, holding a stubby .32 on my middle.

"All right, wise guy," he said, "let's go downtown."

"You sonofabitch," I said. "I'll remember this."

He slapped me across the face with an open palm. I tasted blood.

"Come on, sucker," he said. "Captain Lundeberg wants to see you."

The noose was drawing tighter. I wouldn't have minded, except that it was my neck that was getting squeezed.

12

HEADQUARTERS WAS HOT AND DEPRESSing. I could feel the little rivulets of perspiration running down my back. My insides were bouncing around and I couldn't control them. I kept looking up at the black police squawk-box on one wall, expecting to hear the report of a body found in Griffith Park—woman, young, dark reddish hair. . .

Adam Wheeler came in. He paused to look at me. He started to say something, then stopped. He didn't smile, and neither did I. I held up my handcuffed hands, palms upward, and he only shrugged. He went through a doorway marked PRIVATE.

Presently, the door opened again. Wheeler nodded at the young cop, and the latter came over to me. He said, "Let's go," and led me through the doorway.

A single overhead cord light with a green shield on it hung down from the ceiling. It was swinging back and forth in a slow, ceaseless way. Adam Wheeler straddled a chair beyond it, his hat pushed to the back of his head, his arms crossed over the chair back. Hap Rossi stood near a wall, his smile tiny and bright and mean. The third man in the room was Dan Lundeberg, chief of detectives. He was a big and blond and slat-bodied

Swede with colorless eyes hiding behind rimless glasses and a habit of wanting and getting his own way.

I was in trouble.

The young cop pushed me into a straight-backed wooden chair, then turned and left the room, closing the door behind him.

Lundeberg frowned at my handcuffs. "Get 'em off him," he said.

Rossi strode over to me, unlocked the cuffs, slipped them into his coat pocket. He returned to his original position.

"That's a first-class bastard you got working for you, Lundeberg," I said.

Lundeberg simply looked at me. Nothing changed in his face, but he kept up the steady stare. Finally he got to his feet, slipped out of his suit coat and hung it on the back of his chair. He was wearing bright orange suspenders in addition to his belt. He sat down again and began tracing figure-eights on the top of the desk with a long yellow pencil.

At last he said, "I don't like remarks like that, Phelan. Rossi is an employee of the city. He works hard at his job, and does a good one, too. Trouble with you private dicks is that you've seen too many movies. But I don't like it when you mess in with police business and then act tough with the police." He poked the long yellow pencil at my face. "I don't like it one damned bit."

I said, "I acted tough with Rossi? Ask Rossi."

He sighed. It was a cop sigh. "You've got a good reputation with the police department, Phelan. And you've got a friend in Wheeler, who says you're honest. Rossi doesn't believe you are." He put down the yellow pencil and leaned across the desk, resting on his elbows. "Okay, a guy was found in your car. He had been sapped, and then someone had put two holes in his middle. The holes came from a thirty-eight. Twenty-four hours later, you gave a thirty-eight to Wheeler and the ballistics check shows it's the gun that did the job on Quinn."

Something stuck in my throat—a knot of panic. I tried to clear it out, but it wouldn't budge.

"Okay, Phelan," said Lundeberg. "Your ball."

I opened my mouth, but nothing came out.

Rossi said, "You were in business with Quinn, Phelan. There were hard feelings when you broke up. Why?"

I didn't even bother to look at Rossi; I kept my eyes on Lundeberg. I said, "I told Wheeler I had two witnesses who saw me take that gun off a guy."

"That gun?" It was Lundeberg.

"Yeah, that gun."

Lundeberg opened the top drawer of the desk. He took something out that was wrapped in a soiled white handkerchief. He placed it on top of the desk, and folded back the handkerchief. It was a thirty-eight, a Smith & Wesson, just like the one I had taken from Jimmie Waring.

"Is this the gun?" asked Lundeberg.

I shrugged. "It looks like it."

"In other words, Phelan, you're not positive?"

"No, I'm not. I didn't check the serial number."

"That was pretty dumb of you."

He was right; I couldn't argue that point with him. I had been pretty dumb right along. But I hadn't figured the gun as a plant. I still wasn't sure about it.

Lundeberg said, "You say you have two witnesses that saw you take this gun—" he paused, looked down at the

.38, then up at me again—"a gun, away from someone. Let's go down the line. First, who are the witnesses?"

I told him.

"Harding, the movie star?"

"You know that."

"I just wanted to hear you say it, Phelan. You play around with the big stuff, don't you?"

I didn't answer.

"Who's the other one?"

"Claire Harding's secretary."

"Okay," he said, "could they identify this gun? This particular gun?"

"Only by the appearance of it. They didn't check it any more than I did. You know that, Lundeberg. I don't—"

He interrupted: "I'm disappointed in you, Phelan. You should have had more sense. You are supposed to be intelligent and—" he glanced at Wheeler—"cooperative. Let's see some of that cooperation."

"I handed over the gun, didn't I?"

My words sounded foolish, but Lundeberg didn't smile. "Okay, who was the guy you took the gun from?"

"He said his name was James Waring. He had a couple of business cards in his wallet with that name on it, so I just took it for granted that it was kosher. Apparently, it isn't. He didn't look like the kind that would try to plant a murder gun on me. He said that one of Harding's ex-husbands had hired him to tail her. He said he was broke, and just decided on a stick-up on the spur of the moment. That's when I took the gun away from him."

"A first-class hero," said Lundeberg, and I blushed,

remembering how obviously Waring had kept the safety on the gun.

"You're not saying much."

"No, I'm not."

Lundeberg took a pack of cigarettes out of his shirt pocket. He stuck one in his mouth, then dropped the pack on the desk in front of me. I took one. My hands were shaking when I lit it. The cigarette smoke curled up between us.

I looked over at Adam Wheeler. His eyes were quiet and noncommittal on my face.

I broke the silence. "What are you trying to prove, Lundeberg?"

"I'm not trying to prove anything, Phelan. I don't work that way. I'm trying to solve a murder. A lot of conscience has rubbed off of me in the last seventeen years, Phelan, but I still go through the motions. I'm good at the motions, damned good, and when I want to pin something on a certain guy, I can do it, one way or the other. A dead man is found in your car—the murder gun has your prints all over it. Can you think of a jury that wouldn't convict you?"

"Go to hell," I said.

Rossi laughed. The sound was mean and hard and raked through the room.

"You wise bastards are all alike, Phelan," Rossi said. "You kill me."

"I'll give it some thought," I said.

He reached me in two strides, but this time I was ready for him. He led with his right and I ducked under it, catching him in the pit of the stomach with my left. He grunted harshly, bowing over. I stamped my foot down hard on his instep and he let out a cry of pain. I pushed at his face with the heel of my hand, and he fell over backwards, tumbling against the desk.

Neither Lundeberg nor Wheeler had moved. Lundeberg's impassive gaze remained on my face.

"You're a pretty handy guy, Phelan," said Lundeberg. I didn't answer him.

Rossi groaned. He pulled himself to his feet by holding on to the corner of the desk. He groaned again, and stamped his foot against the floor.

I hoped it would ache him for a week.

Lundeberg said, "That was a dumb play, Rossi. You went for him with a sucker punch."

"I'm sorry, chief."

"Don't apologize for it, for Chrissakes. It's done. Next time you try something like that, finish it." To me, he said, "Sit down, tough guy."

I sat down. Wheeler moved for the first time since I had entered the room. He stood up, reversed the chair, then sat down again, crossing his legs. I got a glimpse of a pair of bright argyle socks and recognized them— I had given them to him last Christmas. Christmas seemed a long time ago.

"Okay," Lundeberg said. "You're not going to cooperate?"

"I'll cooperate to this extent," I said. "I didn't kill Jocko Quinn, and you know I didn't. And I don't know why he was killed, not for sure, not enough to want to spill my beans about it. I don't go off half-cocked, like Rossi."

"What about Harry Dexter?"

I dropped the cigarette on the floor. I looked down at it for a moment, then rubbed it out with the heel of my shoe.

"I don't know," I said.

"He worked for Claire Harding, too," said Lundeberg. "He was found in a wrecked car out on Pico. There was a bottle of booze in the car and Dexter smelled like a week-old drunk. Only thing was, he didn't drink. I've been chasing that one around the block ever since. The only reason I'm letting you go is that it looks like you're next. Maybe we'll get a break with your murder, and clean up the whole damned mess." He paused to probe my face with his hard eyes. "I'm trying to help you, Phelan, but you're throwing it back in my face. Why should I give a damn about you?"

I couldn't answer him. He was right, as far as he went. Only he didn't know about the $250,000, and that made all the difference.

Lundeberg got to his feet. Slowly, and with a great deal of care, he took his coat from the back of his chair, and slipped into it.

"Get him out of here," Lundeberg said. "I don't want to look at him."

He walked out the door.

I stood outside the police building and tried to find some fresh air for my lungs. It was hot and muggy. Two prowl cars darted out of the runway beneath me, their sirens wailing, their red lights blinking, their shielded headlights whitening the night. They skidded around a corner in the distance, and I stood there, listening to the sound of the sirens fading into nothing.

Someone moved on the steps beside me. It was Adam Wheeler. He looked a little unhappy.

"Friend," I said.

"Cut it out, Johnny."

"I like you, too."

He flicked a cigarette to the street; it made a red arch against the night, sparked briefly and rolled into the gutter.

"Let's have a cup of coffee," he said.

"Not tonight."

"Lundeberg's a square guy."

"Sure he is," I said.

"He could have booked you. Maybe he should have. He could have a hell of a time explaining why he didn't."

I said, "Adam, what the hell am I supposed to do? Hop up and down on one leg and sing because he gave me a break? He knows I didn't kill Jocko. What does that make me?"

"It makes you a sorehead, Johnny, the way you're going about it. You could cooperate a little more. It might pay you to do that. That seat you're on right now isn't so damned cool that you couldn't have a little help. The public pays taxes to have murders solved." He paused, then said, "Come on, Johnny, I'll drive you home."

"No," I said. "I've had enough of the police force for one night."

I had no reason to act that way with him. No reason except that I was tired and nervous, angry and—I think —more than a little scared. Someone was doing a good job of slipping a noose around my neck—someone was being pretty smart, much smarter than I.

I hailed a cab. I gave the driver my address.

Adam Wheeler was still standing on the steps of the

police building when I left. He still had that unhappy look on his face.

Dianne Cochran was sitting at the corner window of my apartment when I got there. I closed the door behind me, and breathed deeply—she was the first good thing I had seen that night.

"Hello," she said.

"How'd you get in here?"

"Your landlady let me in. She's nice. I told her I was your cousin." She laughed. "Your landlady's worried about you."

"I'm the kind to worry about."

I looked at the clock on the mantle. Ten thirty-five. Sunday night. Oh, well.

She was wearing a blouse with a low V neck—I had an idea she wanted me to notice it. I noticed it. She straightened the skirt over her knees. The blouse was nice, the skirt was nice, and the knees were nice, too. I slumped down in a chair, and tried to blot out everything else—especially Ellen Quinn—but I didn't succeed.

"Rough day?"

"So-so," I said. "It started out this morning with a breakfast that I cooked myself, burned bacon and greasy eggs. It's been like that all day. I met some lovely people this afternoon, and a few others tonight—servants of the public. Cops to you. You know how they are, don't you? They help old ladies across busy intersections and walk little kids home so the big, bad boogie-man won't get them, and they—" I stopped, feeling idiotic.

She smiled. "You're bitter."

"And you're beautiful," I said. "And did you wear

that dress so I'd knock my eyes out looking?"

"I may have had that in the back of my mind."

She came to her feet to meet me. She made a nice, soft bundle in my arms and I enjoyed doing things with my hands and with my mouth. She seemed to get her kicks out of it, too, but then she put her hands up, pushing me away.

"I need air," she said.

"To hell with it," I said. "You introduced Claire to Harrison Woodward. You didn't tell me that before."

She looked startled. She stepped back, then sat down again, making a production of crossing her legs.

"You have a nasty habit of kissing and then asking questions," she said.

I started to tell her about Ellen Quinn, then stopped. I would keep that one to myself.

"How about a drink?"

"Sure," she said.

I went into the kitchen, rinsed out a couple of glasses, got the ice cubes from the refrigerator, and mixed a couple of strong ones.

I went back ino the other room. I gave her her drink, and slumped down in a chair. She kicked one foot up in the air and her shoe dropped off; a little puff of dust rose from the carpet.

She sipped at her drink. "It's good," she said.

"Sure it is," I said. "Special, just for you."

She laughed; it came from deep within her.

She stood up, did a few dance steps, and her other shoe came off. She stood before me in her stocking feet and laughed again. She took a sip of her drink.

"What the hell do you want?" I asked.

"I want everything, and nothing."

"Make some sense."

"All right—this is a crummy apartment," she said.

"It's all I can afford, baby."

"Do you call them all that?"

"What?"

"Baby?"

"Sure," I said. "It's part of my line."

She laughed again. It was beginning to wear thin on my nerves. I finished my drink in two gulps and went for more. I made it darker this time. I intended to get drunk, good and drunk, and blot out everything.

She wasn't there when I got back in the other room. The way I felt, I didn't mind—but I was only kidding myself. She had been getting under my skin. Then I saw the shoes by the couch; they were placed very neatly, side by side, right in my view. The bedroom door was slightly ajar, but no light showed from in there. I looked at the drink in my hand, then put it down.

The drunk could wait. I walked to the bedroom door. Here goes everything and nothing, I thought.

I could hear her moving around in the bathroom and made an effort to reach the bedside alarm clock. I didn't quite make it, and gave up.

Presently, the light clicked on, and I tried to shield my eyes from the glare. I let my arm fall away and looked at her. She was standing in the middle of the room, deeply tanned all over, and her short hair was mussed and pushed around on her head like a gamin's. There was nothing in her face, absolutely nothing.

She moved over to a chair and started dressing.

I sat up. She came over and I did a zipper up the back for her.

She turned around, cupping my face in her hands. She stared into my eyes for a long time, then kissed me gently on the mouth.

"You won't believe me, John Phelan," she said, "but I love you."

"No," I said. "I don't believe you."

She moved away. It was a sudden, jerky move. She combed her hair in front of the mirror, then turned to me again.

"I do love you, John," she said.

I didn't answer. I just sat there. I couldn't think of anything to say, and didn't particularly want to say anything.

I heard the door shutting from the other room.

I finally got a look at the clock. It said 2:40 A.M. I had gotten through Sunday. It had been quite a day.

I lay down again. I couldn't think of anything else to do.

13

THE BODY WAS FLOATING IN DIRTY BATH water. It was a fat body and there were little wrinkles of white skin where more fat had once been—unattractive —part of the hair had been ripped away from the scalp and the tips of the fingers had been burned and then the body squeezed itself into the drain and disappeared and its place was taken by a long and slim and deeply tanned pair of legs circling through the air and with the legs came the high piercing sound of something I couldn't place.

I awoke. The phone kept ringing. It was seven-thirty. I got up and stumbled into the living room and answered the phone.

It was Claire Harding, and she sounded angry, even at that time of the morning.

I said, "Good morning."

She said, "It is not a good morning, for your information. Just what in the hell are you trying to do to me?"

"At seven-thirty in the morning, nothing."

"Don't get smart."

I sat down on the arm of a chair, and thought about being smart. I said, "Me? Impossible."

"I thought you were discreet."

"So?"

She said, "The police were here last night. They asked me a million questions and it was all quite embarrassing. I only hope the studio can keep it out of the papers."

"Keep what out of the papers? What kind of questions?"

"Personal questions. Many of them too personal to suit me. They asked about Harrison and you and Jocko Quinn and Harry Dexter. Just what in the hell gives around here anyway?"

I said, "The police had me downtown last night. They played cat and mouse with me for a couple of hours and I didn't like it all. Remember that little character out at Dianne's cabin Saturday? The gun I took from him happens to be the same one that killed Jocko Quinn. Did the police happen to ask you about Thompson?"

"What about Thompson?"

"The little guy said Thompson hired him. Do you think that's possible?"

"I told you before I wouldn't be surprised at anything Harold would do."

"Murder included?"

"Oh, don't be an ass. He's a funny little man, but he wouldn't have the gumption to trap a mouse. Not him."

There were a lot of people in this world that wouldn't trap a mouse—sometimes, though, they chopped up people. Somebody had killed Quinn, and used Waring to make me the patsy.

"Okay," I said, "I'll call you later."

I had a shower and breakfast, such as it was. After breakfast, I spent twenty minutes calling the three James Warings I could find in the telephone book. One was a plumber in South Gate; another one was a Negro Baptist minister on the east side; and the final one was a dentist in Compton. Nothing there.

I suddenly remembered the piece of scratch paper I had taken from James Waring. It took me five minutes of searching through various coat pockets before I found it, but there it was: SALLY, HO 4-9921.

I dialed the number.

"Bellevue Hotel." The voice was weary.

"Sally, please," I said.

"Sally who?"

"You know Sally."

"I'm afraid I don't."

The line went dead.

I had one more phone call to make. I found a listing for G. Thompson in Topanga Canyon. The operator put me through.

"Thompson speaking."

"Mr. Thompson," I said, "this is John J. Phelan. I—"

I didn't get any further—he interrupted. "I know who and what you are, Mr. Phelan."

"News certainly gets around."

"Sometimes," he said, "it does."

"Mr. Thompson," I said, "I'll get to the point. A man calling himself James Waring was tailing Claire Harding last Saturday afternoon. He said he was doing so at your instructions."

"That's preposterous."

I had thought it might be. "Then you didn't hire him?"

"I definitely did not."

"He had one of your cards in his pocket."

"That doesn't prove anything."

No, it didn't. Nothing seemed to prove anything.

"Do you happen to know him?"

"The name means nothing to me. Of course, in Hollywood, you meet so many people." He paused. Then: "May I ask how you're coming?"

"Coming with what?" I asked.

"With finding out about Harrison Woodward," he said.

"You may ask," I said, "but it won't do you any good."

"I see."

"I don't think you do, but that's all right."

He cleared his throat. "Mr. Phelan, I have to come into town on business today. If it's convenient for you, I'd like to see you."

"I can make it convenient," I said.

"Fine," he said. "How about two-thirty at the Copper Cup on Sunset?"

"I'll be there. What do you want to see me about?"

"I'll tell you that," he said, "this afternoon."

I hung up, then looked up the Bellevue Hotel in the phone book. It was listed in the 1700 block on north Vine, which would put it just above Franklin.

I left the dishes in the sink, the bed unmade and hoped that when I returned there wouldn't be another body in my bathtub. With my luck, I couldn't be sure.

I let the motor idle in the Plymouth while I lit my pipe. A dark-blue '54 Ford four-door sedan was parked down the street. Two guys were sitting in it. Two guys doing nothing but sitting there. They were looking at everything but me. I pulled out from the curbing, slowed down at the corner, and noticed that the Ford was following.

I turned east on Sunset and the Ford kept following me. They could be cops, but they didn't have to be. I turned north on Vermont, then west on Hollywood.

I pulled into a gas station, told the attendant to fill it up, then park it. The Ford was double-parked across the street. Whoever the two guys were, they weren't being very coy about tailing me. I went around behind the office building, ducked through the parking lot, coming out near the Legion Stadium. A cabbie was leaning against the fender of his cab, reading a paper. I gave him the address of the Bellevue Hotel. When we got to Hollywood Boulevard, the gas-station attendant was still putting gas in the Plymouth, and the Ford was still double-parked across the street.

It had been almost too easy.

The Bellevue Hotel was a narrow, old, three-story building, situated between a parking lot and another hotel of similar vintage. The small lobby was crowded with the usual depressing furniture and equally depressing hangers-on. The desk clerk fitted in perfectly with the motif; he was small, thin, ageless, with cunning eyes and restless fingers.

I got out my wallet, flashed the P-I badge in front of his eyes, but not long enough for him to get a good look at it. His feet plopped on the floor and he sat up straight, interested.

"What room's Sally in?" I asked.

"You the guy called before?"

"Uh-huh," I said.

"I told you then I don't know no Sally."

"Come on, buster," I said.

He looked nervously around the lobby. No one was paying any attention to us. He scratched one ear with nervous fingers.

"She's in three-eleven," he said finally. "Look, I don't know for nothing about her though. Get me?"

Sure, I got him.

"Don't bother to call her," I said.

I got in the rickety old self-service elevator and held my breath while it jarred and jolted me up to the third floor.

Three-eleven was the last door on the north side.

I rapped on the door, waited a moment, then rapped again.

"Who's there?" The voice was small and barely audible.

I didn't answer; instead, I rapped again.

"Who is it?"

"Jimmie sent me," I said.

There was a pause, then the door opened.

She was a lot younger than she looked. Hard times had lined themselves around what must have been at one time pretty brown eyes, and she had one of those mouths that is tritely called rosebud. She was wearing a black brassiere, brown slacks shiny with age, high-heeled shoes, and nothing else. Her hair was dark, but it looked as if it had spent a lot of time changing colors.

She pursed her lips at me and opened her brown eyes in a widely innocent stare. I got the idea that was her stock opening gambit with strangers—pursing those lips and widening those eyes.

"All right," she said, "what's the joke?"

"No joke, honey," I said.

"Like hell," she said. She struck a pose with one hand on a hip; I guess she thought it was sexy. "What do you want?"

"A little time."

She stuck her head out the door, looking up and down the hallway. She seemed satisfied at not seeing anyone.

"Jimmie really send you?"

"No," I said.

"I didn't think so."

"I'd still like a little of your time."

"Who gave you my name?"

"I get around."

She studied me for a moment, then said: "Okay, come on in."

I followed her into the room. She moved with one of those swaying movements that the movie makers peddle as the national walk. With her, the effort was wasted.

The room was dreary, as are all rooms in all hotels like the Bellevue. They're made for people on the edge of life. A pulldown bed, unmade, took up the center of the room; a battered mohair rocker of some unknown vintage was crowded between the bed and the closed windows, and the proverbial hotel desk with the proverbial Gideon bible on it completed the furnishings. One window was covered with an old-fashioned pulldown blind, yellow with age; the other window looked out across a short space of some six or eight feet into another room much like the one in which I stood.

She sat down on the edge of the bed, and said, "You don't look like the kind of a guy would buy it."

"No," I said. I flashed the P-I badge again.

She swore. "A cop. My luck."

"You ever been arrested?"

"What do you think?" She laughed. "Stockton, about a year ago."

"I'm looking for a guy," I said. "A guy who calls himself James Waring, only I don't think that's his name."

She gave me a long and careful look, then got to her

feet and walked over to the window, pulling down the blind.

"Lemme see that badge again," she said.

I didn't move.

"You're not a cop, mister," she said. "You better get the hell out of here, right now."

"No," I said, "I'm not a cop. But I am a private investigator and the law in this state allows me to make arrests."

"Go ahead," she said, "arrest me."

"I'd rather you told me where I can find James Waring."

"I don't know anyone by that name."

I sighed.

"Quit kidding me, honey."

"I ain't kidding you, mister."

"He was carrying your name and phone number and two snapshots of you the last time I saw him."

"That don't mean nothing."

"Okay," I said, "have it your way. I had the idea maybe you and this guy were pretty close. I think his life is in danger. I'd like to help him."

"Why would his life be in danger?"

"He did a job for someone last Saturday. I don't think that someone will want him around very long."

"You on the level?"

"As much as I ever am," I said.

She sat down on the bed again, running a hand through her hair.

"He's downstairs in two-oh-four," she said. "His name ain't Waring, it's Warren."

"Thanks, Sally," I said. "I'll forget about you."

"Do just that," she said.

I walked over to the door.

"Mister," she said, "I hope you been honest with me. I like Jimmie. The breaks been against him, but he ain't a bad guy."

I took the stairs down to the second floor. No one answered my knock at 204. I tried the door, but it was locked. The lock was a cinch, one of those old things easily opened by any dime-store skeleton key, and I did just that.

After I got the door opened, I wished I hadn't. I was getting in the habit of finding dead bodies, and I had enough bad habits without that one, too.

This body was quite dead; there was no doubt about it.

I had been too late.

James Waring, or James Warren, or whatever-the-hell his name had been, was swaying gently on the wrong end of a thin wire hanging from an old brass chandelier in the middle of the room. The plaster ceiling was cracked from his weight and the brass chandelier was tilted dangerously at an angle. Warren's feet were only about ten inches from the floor, and an overturned chair was near them.

The picture was clear and precise.

I set the chair upright, using my handkerchief so as not to leave any prints; I had enough trouble without that, too. I got up on the chair. The wire had cut into his throat, leaving a thin tracing of blood; the blood hadn't completely dried as yet. He hadn't been dead long.

Also, there was a small round bruise about the size of a quarter on his left temple. He had been sapped, then hanged, just as Jocko Quinn had been sapped, then shot.

I used the handkerchief to untangle the wire. It was quite a job. I couldn't hold the body and the wire at the same time, so I let the body fall to the floor; it bumped crazily, and rolled over.

I sat down in the old rocker that was an exact duplicate of the one upstairs. I smoked a cigarette, and let my insides come back to normal. I went into the bathroom, flushing the cigarette butt down the toilet. There was nothing in the bathroom but the usual shaving stuff and a toothbrush.

I gave the place the once-over. There was no dresser. The closet held a tan gabardine suit with nothing in the pockets, a couple of dirty white shirts and a roll of dirty socks. There was an imitation leather suitcase on the floor. I brought it back out and opened it. One clean white shirt. Three letters from a Mrs. Hazel Warren, postmarked several months before from Tacoma, Washington. I read the letters; I didn't think he'd mind.

Hazel and the kids would have to get themselves a new provider.

I put everything back the way I'd found it, being especially careful about leaving any prints around.

Good old John J. Phelan. Good old smart guy.

I went down the list.

Number One: Harry Dexter—a "cute" murder, what with the planted whiskey and all, only the murderer hadn't known Dexter too well or he would have known Dexter's drinking habits—but, I guessed, you didn't have to know someone well to murder him.

Number Two: Jocko Quinn—short and to the point; sapped and shot.

Number Three: Ellen Quinn—brutal, distasteful, sadistic.

Number Four: Jimmie Warren—again, short and simple; sapped and hanged.

Number Five: John J. Phelan?

I shuddered inwardly. I was getting spooky at a time when I needed all my wits about me.

I gave the room another going-over, and then left, going back upstairs. Sally answered my knock immediately this time. Disgust showed on her face.

"You got a short memory, mister," she said.

"Warren's not in."

"What am I supposed to do about that?"

I didn't know. I decided to level with her, but not there in the hallway. I pushed past her into the room. She didn't like that, not one bit.

"Say, what the—"

"Warren's dead."

She didn't say anything. She didn't move a muscle for a long, still moment; then she closed the door behind her and leaned back up against it. I could see the tears forming in her eyes; she rubbed her closed fists against them.

I opened both windows for a little air, and sat down in the rocker. It must have been a full three minutes before she spoke.

"How?"

"It wasn't pretty, Sally. I found him when I got downstairs."

"I said how?"

"They hanged him from a chandelier."

She looked up at her own chandelier, then kicked one foot against the cheap carpet.

"How do I know you didn't do it?"

"Would I have come back up here if I had?"

"I don't know," she said. "I guess not."

She slumped across the room, forgetting the swaying hip movement. She lay down on the bed, covering her face with her arms. I didn't move. I didn't speak. I just sat there.

"He was the only guy I ever knew was good to me." She pulled her arms away from her face, sitting up. She looked at me, then out the window, then back at me. She shrugged. "I know you think I'm some kind of a louse, mister—just a common, every-day whore. But he was good to me and I was good to him and we had something a lot of people don't have."

"I know," I said. Everybody's got something special. I felt a little nauseated. "There's nothing we can do about him now, Sally. He's dead. But you could help me find his killer."

She looked at me, and her whole body sagged. "What do you wanna know?"

"Warren had a job last Saturday," I said. "Someone paid him to try a phony stick-up on me, just so I could take a gun from him. That gun was used in a previous murder, and right now I'm not too popular with the local police. I'd like to know who it was that hired him."

"I don't know that," she said. "You got to believe me."

"Didn't he mention anything at all about the job?"

"Only that he thought it was a soft touch. Only that."

That wasn't much.

"No names?"

She shook her head.

"Okay," I said.

I stood up. "The people here at the hotel know you and Warren were connected?"

"I don't think so," she said. "I don't know. Right now, mister, I don't know anything."

"The police will be around," I said. "They'll probably question all the tenants here."

"I won't peep about you," she said. "You just find whoever it was done Jimmie in."

"I'll try," I said.

I took five twenties out of my wallet. I put them on the desk. Big-hearted me. Yeah, real big-hearted. Hell, I could afford it.

She looked from the money up to me.

"Mister," she said, "you seem square."

"Thanks," I said.

"Jimmie did say one thing. He laughed about it. The guy that hired him wore a big hat. You know, like a cowboy. Jimmie thought he was nuts."

Yeah, I knew.

Big-hat sure got around.

14

I TOOK A CAB BACK TO THE GAS STATION on Hollywood Boulevard, and picked up the Plymouth. The attendant told me that a cop had come over right after I had left, asking about me—the cop had been pretty mad about losing me. I told him it was a gag, but he didn't laugh.

I drove to my office. I had just closed the door behind me when the phone rang. It was Jean MacNeece.

"How are you, lover-boy?"

"I'm alive," I said. "And from the way things are going, that's saying quite a bit."

"Yeah," she said, "I saw in the paper where your ex-partner, Quinn, got knocked off. Have anything to do with you?"

"It might," I said.

Jean said, "I've been thinking about you. I'm keeping my ear to the ground, and I think maybe I ran into something this morning that might interest you. I was doing some leg work and ran into Artie Jackson. He's operating a small agency now, but he used to do publicity stuff for some of the bigger studios around town. And I just happened to remember that Artie did a lot of stuff for Woodward when he was making pictures, so

I popped a couple of questions at him. Guess what?"

"I'm guessing."

"In addition to his other vices, friend Woodward also happens to be mixed up in the dope racket."

I put the sandwich down. I took a firmer grip on the telephone.

"Is this on the level, Jean?"

"I got my fingers raised in the best girl-scout tradition," she said. "Artie isn't the kind of a guy that tosses these things around either, Johnny. If he says it's so, why it's so. When he first came to Hollywood, Woodward did a little pushing on the side, but the big brass got wind of it and had a helluva time with him. He renounced all his sins, but it wasn't good enough for the big boys, so they put the sign on him. That's the reason he can't get a job at any of the big studios."

"Is this known around town?"

"Not by many people, it isn't. I guess because of Claire Harding's big name in the business they managed to keep it pretty hush-hush."

I wondered just how hush-hush.

"You're a sweetheart," I said.

"You toss the words around, Johnny-boy," she said, "but I never see any action."

"You will, believe me."

I hung up, and sat there thinking about what she had told me. A pusher. That was one angle I hadn't figured—he didn't look like the type. But what did the type look like?

I had just finished trying to be a master-mind when the office door opened and Lou Chiozza and his ever-present shadow walked in.

"Gents," I said, "to what do I owe this unexpected pleasure?"

Chiozza didn't say anything. He nodded his head at Joey, and the latter came around the desk. I knew what he wanted. I obliged him. I got to my feet, holding my arms out at shoulder level while he gave me the routine search.

"It's a waste of time," I said. "I never carry one."

"I'm a careful guy, that's all," said Chiozza. "Business is business."

"Sure," I said, "but I didn't know we had any business together."

"We have now," he said.

I sat down again. Joey walked over to the door, standing in front of it, his arms crossed over his chest.

"That's a good boy you got there, Lou," I said.

"Joey does his job." Chiozza sighed deeply. He looked around the office, frowning. He walked over to the desk, picked up the empty carton of coffee, regarded it disgustedly, then dropped it on the floor.

"You live a crummy life, shamus," he said.

"I get by."

"Is that enough?"

I shrugged. He could figure it out for himself.

He took a silk handkerchief from the breast pocket of his $250 suit, dusted the seat of my office chair, then sat down in it—he folded the handkerchief neatly before putting it back in place.

"Careful," I said, "a big, bad germ's liable to bite you."

I reached in the top drawer. Joey stiffened against the door and I smiled at him. I took out a pad of paper and a pencil. I wrote on the pad: $250,000. I pushed the pad at Chiozza. He picked it up, looked at it, then put it down again.

"You take chances, Phelan," he said. "That isn't smart."

"That's a matter of opinion," I said.

"The police had you downtown last night. Why?"

"Ask them. You seem to have a pipeline down there."

The smile virtually tore his face in half.

"I'm not a well man, Phelan," he said, "and wise guys like you don't make me feel any better. My ticker don't tick as often as it should, and that worries me. I got to watch my weight and my activity and everything I like to do I can't do."

"I'm feeling for you," I said.

"I'm going to level with you, shamus," he said. He leaned forward, resting his hands on the desk. "I made a business investment in Harrison Woodward. It cost me twenty-five grand initial outlay, but I stood a chance of making a good pile. I don't like to lose twenty-five grand."

"So?"

"So now Woodward's skipped. I can't find him. I think maybe you know where he is."

"You're way off, Lou," I said.

"I want him."

"So do I."

"Don't push your luck too far with me, shamus. I'm not a guy to play with."

"I know what kind of a guy you are." I said. "You're a big man around town. You've got a few bookie joints here and there, not too many, but enough, and I think you've got a line into Vegas. You have protection somewhere along the line, but I don't think you have enough.

If it comes right down to it, guys like you never have enough. You spent time in Quentin and I don't imagine a guy with your tastes in life enjoyed that very much. You might be back in there before too long, if you get any ideas that you can push me around. I've had about enough of that."

"You talk big for such a little jerk, shamus."

"Sure," I said. "But I haven't got your worries. You're tied in with Harrison Woodward, probably more than the twenty-five grand you talk about. Two guys before me tried to figure what Woodward was up to. They're both in the morgue now. The cops are trying those two murders on various people for size, Chiozza, and they might just be interested in your connection with Woodward."

"Joey," he said. Nothing more; just that.

Joey treaded water across the room towards me. I took a quick look at those flat-knuckled hands and the backs of my legs began to ache. I got to my feet and waited for him and he came on like I was nothing at all. When he was about a yard away, I dropped my right hand; his eyes followed the movement, and I brought my left around with the telephone in it and clobbered him right on the side of the head. He tumbled backwards, falling into Chiozza. He and Chiozza and the chair all went to the floor together. I walked around the side of the desk and kicked Joey right on the point of the chin.

He wouldn't bother me for a while.

Chiozza climbed to his feet. His face was a shade grayer and his breath was coming in short, heavy gasps. He looked at me, then at Joey. He mumbled something under his breath and kicked the unconscious Joey in the stomach. He smiled.

"He's a good boy, Lou," I said, "but he's punchy. He

can't think, and I'm beginning to believe you can't either."

"That's that?" he said.

"You're damned right it is," I said.

He picked the chair up and sat down in it. He took a long cigar from his inner pocket and stuck it in his mouth. He lit it, savoring the smoke.

"I get three of these a day," he said. "Christ. When I was a kid on the east side I used to dream of growing up some day and making a pile so I could really live it. You know how a kid is, big dreams about fancy cars and fancy foods and hot dames and all that. And now I got the dough, but no health." He laughed.

"That's too damned bad," I said.

"Yeah," he said.

His hands were shaking.

"You find Woodward for me," he said, "and ten percent of the twenty-five grand is yours."

"I've got one client," I said.

"Take on another."

"I don't work that way."

Joey groaned. He moved to a sitting position, shaking his head from side to side. I bent over him briefly, removed the gun from his shoulder clip. There was a raw red spot on the side of his chin where I had kicked him. I matched it with another kick. He slumped back down without a sound.

I don't know why I did that. Jean had said Woodward was mixed up with dope. Chiozza had admitted being mixed up with Woodward. Joey was Chiozza's muscle, and we could never have been pals, anyway.

"He won't like you when he wakes up," said Chiozza.

"That'll break me up," I said. "Now pick him up and carry him the hell out of here."

Chiozza squinted at me. His eyes were all mixed up, but mostly they held hate.

I said, "Get going." I still held Joey's gun.

He tried a smile. "You want to do this to me, Phelan? I told you about my bum ticker—you want to kill me?"

"It's an idea," I said, and watched him bend over finally, and begin to tug at Joey.

15

THE COPPER CUP, AT THE WEST END OF the Sunset Strip, tried very hard to be a bit of Old England and only succeeded in being a bit of new Hollywood. The usual crowd of happiness boys and girls was at the bar. The conversations were all fast, loud, about the movies and punctuated with pointing forefingers. I received a few inquisitive stares and immediate dismissals.

I gave my name to the hostess.

The man in the booth didn't bother to rise. He had a thin face and darkish-green eyes, dulled by time and liquor. He was wearing a tan corduroy jacket, a polka-dot bowtie, a gray mustache, and a fixed smile.

"Sit down, Mr. Phelan," he said. His voice was lower than it had been on the phone, lower and cultured.

I sat down, ordered a beer—he took the opportunity to order another martini. It was pretty early in the day for too many of those.

"You wanted to see me about something?"

He ignored that. "I allow myself the maximum of two good drunks per month. This happens to be one of the times that I'm heading in that direction."

The waitress brought our drinks. She placed them on copper-colored napkins shaped like cups, then left.

I said again, "You wanted to see me, Thompson."

"Of course," he said.

A tall redhead in a dark sweater and dark slacks approached the table; she had overly large breasts and was putting them to good use in that sweater.

"Harold, darling," she said to Thompson.

It was the first time he had stopped smiling.

"Hello, Mira," he said.

"How's that script coming, darling? Are you up-grading that part of mine?"

"I'm writing in a special scene," he said, "in which you wear nothing more than a bikini."

Mira's eyes lit up. "I'll kill the bastards. I'll absolutely kill 'em."

"That you will, Mira," Thompson said.

"You are a sweet darling," Mira said.

She bent down, kissed Thompson on the cheek. She gave me a smile and a wink, and undulated away. I watched her slide into a booth opposite us, to join a young man in a Brooks Brothers suit and an intense look. She leaned across the table, whispering something to him, and they both looked over at Thompson and me, laughing.

"Don't mind the laughter, Mr. Phelan," Thompson said.

"I don't get you."

"They're having a good laugh at our expense, Mr. Phelan," he said. "You and me. You see, the word around this godforsaken village is that I'm—peculiar. Mira has just informed her intense young friend of that fact and, as a result, you must join me in being the butt of a very dirty, very sordid, and very untrue joke."

"I've heard the rumor," I said.

"Have you?"

He appraised me with a new and sincere look. He studied the martini before him, then took half of it in one gulp.

"Don't worry though," he said. "For what it's worth, I'm perfectly normal in all aspects."

I said, "If you want to blurt out all your little problems, I would suggest a psychiatrist. I'm a detective."

"Quite so," he said.

He finished the martini, then signaled for the waitress to bring us another round.

"How is the case progressing, Mr. Phelan? I think case is the appropriate term, isn't it?"

"It's the right term," I said. "And I gave you your answer this morning. It still stands."

He shrugged. He folded his napkin up into a little paper ball and began playing soccer with it between his two forefingers. It was an uninteresting game.

"Mr. Phelan," he said. "I'm interested in helping you."

"Why?"

"Why?" He thought about that, then laughed. "I'm about to make a confession to you—I'm still in love with Claire. It's hopeless, I know, but there it is. I don't deny that she is a bitch, either. But I want her to be as happy as she possibly can in this crazy world, and I believe, by helping you, I might be helping her."

"In what way would you help me?"

"She hired you to find out about her present husband, why he has been stealing from her. I know the reason."

"You're not telling me anything yet," I said. "I know the reason he took the stuff. But what I don't know is from whom he got a quarter of a mill—"

Thompson wasn't listening to me. He wasn't quite aware of anything at that moment. His face was frozen into a solid mask of terror. He sat there, not moving, then suddenly his shoulders began twitching and he pulled his lips back from his teeth and spittle spilled out of the corner of his mouth.

I turned in the direction of his stare. I couldn't see anything or anyone other than the crowd at the bar and the hostess and the cashier talking together.

I got out of the booth and strode to the bar. The people were crowded together; the talking was a constant clatter in the air. A stout man in a gray pin-stripe suit moved away from the congestion. He had a moon-round face, dark like a Mexican's or a South American's and a small brown cigarillo stuck in his mouth.

I turned, looking back at Thompson. He was running down the aisle between the booths, heading for the back door. I started to follow. A hand grabbed me roughly by the shoulder and then something hard hit me in the back of the head and then it was like it always is . . .

It always scares the hell out of me.

16

I COULD HEAR THE VOICES, BUT I couldn't make out what was being said. It didn't matter much anyway. Something soft was under my head, and then the gray began to soften a little and I could see. Not clearly, and I shut my eyes.

A voice said, "I don't know. I couldn't catch up with him. He ducked down the alley."

Another voice said, "Welch won't like this."

The first voice agreed with the second voice.

I wondered who Welch was.

There was the sound of someone dialing a telephone, then the second voice said, "Mr. Welch, please. . . Edwards here, sir. We trailed Thompson to a bar on Sunset where he met Phelan. Garcia came in later and frightened him away. There was a scuffle and Phelan got hit over the head. We're in the back office of the bar now, waiting for Phelan to come out of it." A pause. "No sir, they both got away." Still another pause. "Yes sir, I know, I'm sorry." The phone clicked back to its cradle.

"So what does he want us to do now?" It was the first voice again.

"He wants us to bring Phelan in. He's sending other details out to Topanga and Santa Monica. How's Phelan?"

"I don't know. That's a nasty crack behind his ear."

I cracked my eyes open and the gray was gone. A strong hand raised my head and something hot was forced between my lips. It burned going down, but it did the job.

I looked around. I was in an office. I could see a desk and a man sitting behind the desk and, behind the man, above his head, a ridiculous painting in too-bright colors of a figure in a red jacket on a horse jumping over a high bush with water beneath it.

I sat up. The back of my head ached dully.

The man standing above me was tall and young and dressed in a conservative, single-breasted brown suit.

"He gave you a real wallop," the man in the brown suit said.

I didn't have to have him tell me that.

I looked across the room at the other one. He stood up and drummed his fingers against the top of the desk. He, too, was tall and young; he, too, was dressed in a conservative, single-breasted suit—his was gray.

I asked, "What's going on?"

Brown-suit flashed a wallet in front of my eyes, just enough for me to see his identification. It was good enough for me. It always would be.

I stood up, fighting the dizziness.

"Don't try to rush it," Brown-suit said.

I put my hand to the back of my head, found a lump the size of a walnut behind my ear, but there was no blood. I guess I could be thankful for that. "What now?"

"You're coming with us."

"Where?"

"Never mind that."

"I take it the guy that conked me got away?"

Gray-suit nodded.

"And Thompson, too?"

He nodded again.

"Some help you guys are," I said. I tried to make it sarcastic, but it didn't come off.

Brown-suit took hold of my arm. We went out of the office and up the aisle between the booths and the bar. The conversational hum ceased when we walked by and someone yelled, in a high, shrill voice, "Boys will be boys", and the laughter started low and then spread; it followed me outside. It might have been funny to someone. It wasn't to me.

The sunshine was too quick and too bright. Brown-suit and I got into the back seat of a cream-colored Mercury while Gray-suit got into the front seat.

He drove east on Sunset to LaBrea, then south to Wilshire, then east again. We parked near the corner of Wilshire and Western, and I was vaguely conscious of the theatre marquee that juts out over that busy intersection—the letters were two feet high and spelled out that Claire Harding was still starring in FOREVER YOU.

Forever was getting to be a damned long time for her.

We entered an office building beside the theater and took the elevator to the sixth floor. The sign on the door read MARTIN J. WELCH, INVESTMENTS.

The room was small and crowded with three or four pieces of standard-looking office furniture. You would never guess what really went on there—at least, I wouldn't. There was another door in the opposite wall marked PRIVATE.

A blonde with a cool and efficient look was sitting behind a small desk with a typewriter on it, absently cleaning her fingernails. She looked up when we came in and said, "Go on in. He's expecting you."

The second room was much larger than the first. There were three men in it, and two of them I knew—Adam Wheeler and Dan Lundeberg.

It was the third man in the room who bothered me. Martin J. Welch had been the name on the door. He was leaning against the edge of the desk, looking down at Lundeberg when we came in. His head jerked upright and he gave me a long and unkind look. His eyes were bright blue, set in deep sockets. He looked as if he might have been a good blocking back for Notre Dame in the late thirties. He looked like a lot of man.

He brushed right by me and ushered Brown-suit and Gray-suit out of the office. I stood there and tried not to think of anything and found that it was amazingly simple when you put your mind to it.

Lundeberg spoke first. "I had two men on you, Phelan. You gave them the slip this morning."

I didn't say anything.

"How's the head, Johnny?" asked Wheeler.

I smiled at him. "I wish I knew how you meant that, Adam."

Wheeler's mouth twitched.

The big man with the deep-set blue eyes came back into the room. He stopped beside me. His eyes swept my face and then he surprised me by sticking out a huge hand.

"I'm Martin Welch," he said. "Special investigator for the Bureau of Narcotics."

I gripped the hand. It was strong; it conveyed purpose. He shoved a chair against the backs of my legs and I sat down.

"This is going to take some time, Phelan," he said. "I hope you don't mind."

I said I didn't.

Welch walked around behind the desk, sat down. He said, "I have no legal right to detain you, Phelan."

"I figured that," I said.

"Do you want to cooperate?"

"I'll do what I can."

"Fine," he said. "Fine." He leaned back in the chair, cupping his hands behind his head, staring up at the ceiling. "First, I'm going to tell you a little story. I think it might impress you, and I want it to do so. Some three months ago, a buyer for a European syndicate came to this country with two hundred and fifty thousand dollars to buy a batch of heroin that was being held here. There was a middleman in the deal, a man who handled the transaction for both the buyer and the seller. We knew, beforehand, of this pending deal, but allowed it to develop for two reasons—we wanted to learn the identity of the middleman, and the location of the heroin. The money passed from the buyer to the middleman, but we still hadn't located the heroin, and then the unforeseen happened. The middleman decided to cross the sellers and keep the payoff for himself. He needed money to cover himself for a short time and, as he had a wealthy wife, he began selling some of her valuables. At a certain time he was going to pack up and leave, with a certain person, a quarter-million dollars richer.

"However, his wife grew suspicious and hired a private investigator to find out why her husband was stealing from her. One thing led to another. The private investigator found out more than was good for him, and so he had to be disposed of. The wife then hired a second investigator. This one was somewhat smarter than the first, with the result that he not only found out more than he should have, but he also did something about it." Welch removed his hands from behind his head, and leaned forward. "This second private investigator stole the quarter-million, knowing that the people from whom he had taken it could not go to the proper authorities and report the loss. It would have worked, maybe, except that the middleman then went to the sellers and told them the money had been hijacked from him. The sellers tracked down the thief. He was done away with, naturally, but the money had disappeared. Which, Mr. Phelan, brings us up to you."

I lit a cigarette and said, "I don't have the money—or the heroin—if that's what you want."

"We've got the heroin now, and we know you don't have the money."

"Well, then?"

He rose to his feet, stretched, then sat down again. He smiled.

"We've already picked up Woodward," he said, "who, as you probably have guessed by now, was the middleman with the big ideas. The man you met this afternoon at the Copper Cup, Harold G. Thompson, was a user. He was ready to inform, I think because of his former wife."

"I still don't know what you want from me."

"I'm getting to that," he said. "Lou Chiozza was in on the deal with Woodward, and so was one other person, the woman with whom Woodward was going away. We know her name, Helen Bethke, but we know nothing else about her. We have a description and some pictures of her, and that's all. We've had men parked across the street from her apartment with a camera, taking hundreds of feet of film, but we've never been able to get a clear face shot. We took a risk with her, letting her run free until the last minute, and now she's skipped." He smiled again. "I hate to admit defeat."

"I still don't understand where I fit in."

"You've worked hard on this case, Phelan. You're an experienced operator. Maybe you've stumbled across something that we've missed. It's possible."

Yes, it was possible.

"We have an alert out for Thompson now," he said. "Also for Luis Garcia, the man who hit you over the head in the Copper Cup. He works for the sellers in the East and South America. He and a man we only know by the name of Bruno are the hatchet-men for the sellers. Damned good ones, too, if I do say so."

"Yeah," I said. "Would friend Bruno be a tall guy that wears a ten-gallon hat and makes like a cowboy?"

Welch nodded.

He said, "Don't get the idea they can escape us permanently. It's just a matter of time before we pick them up. What makes matters a little pressing is the money. We'd like to pick that up intact."

"Okay," I said. "I'll tell you what I know."

Welch brought in the blonde secretary to take down my statement. I began at the beginning and told them the whole thing, right from the first time I had seen "Daddy" drunk in Claire Harding's house. My voice droned out into the room and my throat got dry, but I kept at it. Both Welch and Lundeberg kept interrupting me, asking me question after question, popping them at me until my head was swimming with them. I even told them about finding Ellen Quinn's body in my bathtub.

It was something they didn't know about. Lundeberg didn't like it, not one bit. He ripped at me for taking the body to Griffith Park. The body had been found, but not identified as yet. I told them about James Warren and the way I found him at the Bellevue Hotel. They had known I had been there—the desk clerk had given them my description. I told them about every damned thing that had happened to me since Friday morning.

Almost.

After that, we went into a projection room. I looked at more feet of film than I had seen in the movies in the past two years. More questions. More film. There were shots of the apartment building at 709 Crescent Way, of many people coming and going; I saw myself talking to the pimply-faced kid next door, going into 709, coming out again; I wasn't much of an actor—in fact, I was lousy. I saw Harold G. Thompson, and identified him; I saw Harrison Woodward, and identified him; I saw the stout guy with the moon-round, dark face, and identified him. I saw them all. I saw too much.

Some time, during that long seige of darkness and the many, many questions, something registered deep within me— it was not enough. It had to lie there awhile . . .

Finally I stood outside in the hallway, smoking my last cigarette. Welch stood in front of me, looking like a football coach whose team is trailing by at least three touchdowns at halftime.

"That's all?" he asked.

"That's it," I said.

"Okay," he said. He paused, not looking at me. "You had ideas about that money, didn't you?"

"Sure," I said. "Why not?"

"It wouldn't have done you any good."

"You'd be surprised," I said.

"No," he said. "You would have been, though."

I didn't get him.

"You see," he said, "the money is counterfeit. It's not worth a damn." He smiled. "That's why we're so anxious to get it all back. It's very good counterfeit, and it could hurt the wrong people."

That got me. That, and everything else, too.

It was dark outside when they let me go. I didn't know what time it was. I didn't much care. Not then. Somebody drove me home and I had a hell of a time getting up the stairs to my apartment. My hand was shaking when I put the key into the lock. I had barely made my bedroom when the telephone began ringing. I didn't move a muscle.

Finally it stopped.

I don't know how long I slept. But when I woke up, the pattern was amazingly clear and in place.

I sat up. I saw my living quarters through someone else's eyes. *A crummy little place.* It cost me $82.50 per month, and it wasn't worth that.

A crummy little life. Maybe.

I knew what I had to do.

I dressed, called a cab, then went downstairs to wait for it. It was still dark, but I could see the clouds moving ever so slowly high in the sky, and way off in the west I could hear the distant rumble of thunder, which is an unusual thing for Los Angeles. But then, I didn't expect to have many awakenings like this.

I gave the cabbie the address of the Copper Cup. The rented Plymouth was still where I had parked it. I got into it and drove west on Sunset, turned north at the ocean, going towards Malibu. The little MG made a dull red glow beside the highway. I went right on past it and stopped at the first gas station. I made a phone call. It didn't take long.

I drove south again and parked behind the MG. I stood there and looked at it for a moment and asked myself if I could be sure—and I knew I couldn't back down now.

I walked down the narrow space between the cabins. The door was unlocked. I opened it, stepped inside.

She was sitting there with that pretty face of hers, beside the french doors.

"Darling," she said, "what—"

"Never mind," I said.

She gave me a too-quick smile and got to her feet. She came quickly across the room to meet me and I let her do that much. She was still desirable to me. Something started way down deep inside me and I had to fight against it.

"You look tired, sweetheart," she said.

"I am tired," I said.

"Poor darling."

My slap stung her face. She recoiled from me.

I said, "Why?"

It was only one word, but it told her. Her body stiffened and she backed away from me, holding her hands behind her . . .

Much later I asked her the question again, and she sighed. "I don't know why, darling, not really. I guess it began when I met Harrison for the first time. I was eighteen. He was worldly and charming and he was the first man I ever gave myself to, wholly. I fell in love with him. He used me, but I didn't mind, then. He was mixed up in narcotics in Europe, too, but things got too warm for him, so, when he met Claire, he shifted to this country. I suppose I could blame Claire, but I won't. My up-bringing wasn't really a helluva lot, John—but I never used the stuff myself. I saw what it did to others."

"It's over now," I said.

"Maybe," she said. "Maybe it is, maybe it isn't. It doesn't have to be."

"No," I said, "it doesn't."

"I don't love Harrison any more. That was over a long time ago, but by then I was in too deep to back out. Besides, Johnny—a quarter-million—now I've got the chance to get out and stay out. And I told you the truth the other night, darling."

"Yes?"

She said, "I do love you."

"Of course," I said. And for the same quarter-million it could have been Harrison Woodward.

We didn't say anything for a while. There was just the sound of the ocean moving outside.

"I have the money here, darling," she said. "We can go away, together. Just the two of us. We could have a good life together."

"Sure," I said.

We both heard the footsteps at the same time. She didn't move a muscle. She just stood there, looking at me. There was a lot in that look. I still wake up in the middle of the night and see it; I can't rid myself of it.

They came in the door, two nameless guys in conservative, single-breasted suits and Martin Welch and Adam Wheeler.

They led her out of the cabin and she never looked at me again. Adam Wheeler came up to me, putting a hand on my shoulder, squeezing it slightly. He shoved a pack of cigarettes under my nose. I shook my head.

"How'd you know, Johnny?"

"I told Welch," I said. "It registered on me after I got home. There was never a clear picture of her, Adam, but there were a lot of shots of her body and her back. I know that body."

I turned, listening to the footsteps receding in the night. Martin Welch was systematically searching the cabin, searching for the money. It didn't take him long to find it. It was wrapped in brown paper, and he brought it over, unwrapping it. I looked down at the money. A quarter-million made quite a pile.

"Thanks, Phelan," Welch said.

His face was wreathed in a big smile; his team had come from behind at the last moment.

"She was damned clever," I said.

"They're all clever, Johnny," said Wheeler.

Sure, they were.

I walked to the windows and looked out over the ocean. The thunder continued to rumble in the distance and a ship's horn blasted its answering challenge.

I stood there, and just looked.

It was a nice night.

Yeah, it was.

THE END

www.ingramcontent.com/pod-product-compliance
Lightning Source LLC
Chambersburg PA
CBHW030230180626
46810CB00008B/3053